ALGO

A STORY OF LOVE AND ALGORITHM

CASEY MILONE

www.caseymilone.com

*This book is dedicated to the
women and non-binary people
in my life, both past and present.
Specifically my mother for caring
for me during the darkness, my
former partner for supporting
my creativity unconditionally, my
nibbling for making me excited
about the future, and my wife
without whom I would never have
found myself.*

CONTENTS

INTERNATIONAL DISTRICT

Hanna forgot his name immediately after she sat down—something her date's OS would never let him do. Along with her name, age, consent indicator, and any past STI treatments, it would be pulling on her search history and displaying the results in his lenses. No doubt the information was floating around her face with some design he paid a stylist to curate. You could learn a lot about someone from their search history and he would want to verify that she subscribed to the same version of geopolitical events as his peers. It would be super embarrassing for him to bring some nationalist truther home for dinner with his network of academically inclined lovers.

People didn't so much go on dates anymore. That was a social construct demanding a level of commitment that flew in the face of modern sexual behavior. Now, in an era valuing expedient and malleable connection, Hanna's generation preferred polyam arrangements based on mutually expressed consent. As a cultural shift, it suited her. She had always been a person comfortable with—and often preferring—non-binary romantic entanglement. But polyamory had become intertwined with data overlay tech due to the communication efficiency it offered, and Hanna was sick of knowing so much about someone so quickly.

"So... you don't wear lenses?"

"I don't wear lenses on first dates," Hanna replied.

"But your haptics are on?"

"Nope."

"That must make meeting people really weird."

"This conversation usually does the trick."

"How do you verify someone's search history? Shit, how do you signal changes in consent?"

"I do those things by talking," Hanna said.

"But you *do* own lenses, right?" This last probe seemed to be about her financial situation.

"I work as a design lead at Moshi Moshi. My work requires that I use them, so yes."

"Oh? That's a cool agency." He looked visibly relieved.

"Yeah, we do some interesting work if you're into that kind of thing. What did you say you do again?" A question she wouldn't need to ask if she'd bowed to convention and put in her lenses.

⹀

Walking away from the cafe after paying for both of their drinks to prove a point, Hanna grabbed a vending wall corned sim-beef sandwich and headed back to the office. Peeling back the origami wrapper, she bit into it as she walked. No one ate bio-beef anymore. It had even fallen out of favor with the wealthy of Seattle. The carbon impact was just too great, and plant-based imitations had become so good that it was impossible to justify— not to mention the havoc it would wreak with your search history. Hanna had met people who were into raising and eating chickens. They spun a story about being freegan and self-sustaining—odd to be sure, but a moral high ground could be found there. With one's purchases, dining reviews, fitness predilections, medical logs, and search activity trailing behind them for all to see, there wasn't room for a sociological misstep in the 80s.

This train of thought reminded Hanna that she was walking blind. She drew the small bottle from her shoulder bag and popped it open between bites of corned sim-beef. Squirting the liquid lenses into each eye prompted her OS to wake up and she fell hard into a world of mixed reality.

The landscape flooded with signage as she walked uphill from the International District. They looked like billboards and storefront signs hanging from the sides of buildings she walked by, but they were all algo-curated, predicting her interests with frightening accuracy. Advertisers bid against each other in an automated auction vying for an impression as she walked back to work. Her own OS was left with the job of predicting whether she actually needed to see the signs of physical businesses she passed, weighing the value of her interest in the world around her against the microtransactions trickling into her bank account as she viewed the ads.

The mixed reality advertising saw her too, in its own way. Biometric nanofibers woven into everything she owned tracked her heart rate and imperceptible changes in her body temperature while her lenses took note of her pupil dilation and eye movements. All this was fed back into the dataset fueling Alphabet's algo, powering their ever-improving ad targeting.

Keeping with the generations-long tradition of trading personal data for indispensable function, the biometric information streaming from her clothing was also the basis for her personal OS. The software sitting at the center of every person's life was made by a few different companies, but the differences in the way they worked was superficial. Hanna lived with an AI companion. One that inhabited the background of every interaction, love affair, work project, purchase, and travel plan she had. It wasn't an anthropomorphized caricature with a name and a contrived personality. It lived in the shadows of her life, predicting anything she may need in the moments before she realized she needed it. And it did this by studying her search history and interpreting her live biometric information, something its designers had taught it to do with the training data from generations of people around the globe. Hanna doubted that anyone really knew how a personal OS did what it did anymore. As was the way when working with an algo, all people could offer was the dataset, the parameters, and the expectation for an output. How the AI solved for that output was impossible to know. Something that only scared the shit out of her once or twice a year. What she did know was that her personal OS was built on an unshakable foundation of privacy and the data it passed off to the mixed reality advertisers was anonymized and one-way.

She had picked the location of her coffee date so that it would be walking distance to her gym. Rather than compressing her twenty-four-hour work week into three days like many of her coworkers, Hanna liked to take a few hours to herself in the middle of each day. Early in her fitness journey she had fallen in with the VR immersion crowd, running in a full haptic bodysuit on a three-dimensional treadmill through imaginary historical landscapes— placing giant stones to build the pyramids, digging trenches during combat in Vietnam, getting yelled at while rowing crew at Harvard. These days though, she had come full circle to the lowest-tech workout in the city: obstacle course running. She first came across this gym during a team building activity through work, but where everyone else thought it was a novelty Hanna came back the next day, bruised and sore, to sign up.

The workout was modeled after some turn-of-the-century television show from her grandparent's era. It was a series of platforms, rope swings, climbing nets, hanging bars, and a fourteen-foot curved wall that she still couldn't climb. After a warm up, she stood at the beginning of the course visualizing her run. The other core function of her OS was the ability to modulate her emotional experience by flipping the flow of biometric info inwards and using her clothing to make subtle suggestions to her heart rate, breath, and body temperature. The practical upshot of this was that she could turn her emotional experiences up and down at will (something she could have used to get through her frustrating coffee date). All of these interactions between her and her OS happened with a silent understanding. Her OS just knew what she was after at all times. It would be creepy if it wasn't so intrinsic to modern life.

Hanna turned down her nervous energy and ran. Leaping from one angled platform to the next then grabbing a rope swing that terminated in a leap to the underside of a hanging net. She missed with one hand on the net and fell hard to the mat below knocking the wind out of her. Standing at the starting platform for a second time, she went in the other emotional direction and dialed up the adrenaline from the fall. This time she made it through the course and found herself standing at the final obstacle. The giant wall curved inward to make a vertical ramp she was meant to run up before leaping to its top ledge and pulling herself up. Bent over, Hanna took a few breaths to recover and threw herself at it, running up the wall. Her fingers grasped at the lip. They slipped, sending her back down to a sliding stop on her knees.

"Fuck!" she yelled into the cavernous gym, turning a few heads.

She reset her haptics, removing the emotional modulations she had in place for her workout and hit the showers. Her recent experiment with putting her OS to sleep on first dates came from a growing frustration. A sense that she was missing out on one of life's lost treasures. The results were inconclusive so far.

DOWNTOWN

Heading back into the office, Hanna walked along 3rd Street and looked at the abandoned buildings rising out of the water to her left. Seattle's downtown was a series of steep hills that dove straight into the lapping waves of Puget Sound. When it came time to make the hard choices about rising sea levels, the city had cut its losses and abandoned some real estate rather than building and maintaining the kinds of seawalls found in New York and the Bay Area. While the waterline was only up by a matter of inches around the world, the changing weather over the last eighty years meant that a lot of coastline had been lost to regular storms before its time. The lack of a seawall in Seattle meant the flooding of a historic neighborhood, but that kind of loss had been felt on every coastal state many times over.

The Moshi Moshi office was a tinted glass box wedged into the side of an older high-rise across from the Seattle Public Library. The silver lattice of the library's exterior was reflected in its windows. The office was empty and white on the inside, just a bunch of unassigned desks, meeting rooms, and working walls for design reviews. Walking in, Hanna tossed her bag into a chair where her team usually hung out. Looking around, she saw them standing in a group facing a blank wall. As she walked over to join them, they added her to the scrum and the content they were sharing flooded the wall in front of her. The wall was littered with scraps of people's recent digital nomading, heavily filtered food porn, and pets. She brushed the clutter away with a gesture, and the contents of her own shared folder populated, dancing in with an animation chosen by her stylist.

She selected a filegroup and a slow-moving river made from hundreds of logos streamed across the wall. This style of generative design output was based on some neurological principle or another meant to facilitate thin-slicing. Hanna's OS tweaked the haptics in her clothing, helping to regulate her breathing, dropping her into a mindfulness practice she'd specialized in during design school. The team softened their gazes, letting their adaptive unconscious formulate opinions. The algo trimmed the torrent of options down to something they could wrap their heads around as they reviewed them.

Xin-Lao was the first to speak. "There's a definite masculine lean in these." They had a short, asymmetrical haircut, and their small frame was tented in an oversized coat with architectural lines. The surface of the coat shifted and shimmered with animated graphic design—always threatening to resolve into something the brain could identify, then slipping away.

They weren't wrong. The Moshi Moshi algo had picked up on something in the ocean of data surrounding the client and was pushing these designs in the direction of the automotive industry from Hanna's grandparent's generation. Feelings of unbidden progress, forward-slanting angles, independence.

"Yeah. Weirdly retro, huh?" Hanna replied.

After the meeting, Hanna was surprised to find Xin-Lao walking back to the team desks with her. Although they had been working together for the better part of a year, Hanna didn't know a lot about Xin-Lao. They were blindingly competent. That much was clear. In the organizational structure of their team, Hanna was senior, but since Xin-Lao wasn't her direct report, they interacted like peers. The two of them paused before parting ways and smiled at each other.

"Would you like to grab a drink after work?" Xin-Lao asked casually.

Hanna was envious. As if stepping outside of one's friend network was as simple as trying a new pastry. "Ummm... yes. Sure. That sounds lovely," she replied.

Xin-Lao walked away, and Hanna spent the rest of the afternoon teasing apart the encounter.

=

Later the two of them sat in a perfectly constructed blend of hipster tech meets turn-of-the-previous-century apothecary. They ordered artisanal cocktails and a forty-three-dollar bowl of olives. The place was so perfectly constructed for their demographic that every menu item looked good, its cocktail specials curated with hyper-local behavioral data.

As they sat there, it dawned on Hanna that this was a date. Before her OS could start to pull information about Xin-Lao and pile it around their face, Hanna blinked twice in the universal signal for OS sleep, then she took out her lenses. Xin-Lao noticed and looked bemused. Then, without a word, they did the same.

"Fun," they said.

Hanna smiled, blushing unexpectedly and immediately missing her haptics.

"How do you feel about this place?" Xin-Lao asked, their coat now showing what looked like live weather patterns over the Pacific.

"I don't know. It's nice, I guess. The menu seems well put together. I like the decor. Why? You want to go somewhere else?"

"No. I mean does it make you feel any particular way? Were you excited to come check it out?"

"I... no, I guess I wasn't," Hanna replied.

"When was the last time you remember feeling seriously excited about a new restaurant or boutique or live VR serial—whatever it is that turns you on? I don't know you well enough to guess at what that would be. What's your thing? What do you nerd out on?"

"I love food, actually. This place should be right up my alley."

"But there's no otaku."

"What?"

Xin-Lao smiled.

"The Japanese word 'otaku' dates to the 1980s. It was a derogatory term for anime and manga nerds. Then it was taken back by the nerd kingdom and co-opted into something positive. In the first thirty years of this century, otaku was used to describe people with unfettered fandom—people lining up for new pastries in Manhattan, watching *Naruto* until they got bedsores in Berlin, driving across Tokyo to try a new variety of ramen—you name it. It became a way to describe those with a singular passion that drove them to the point of obsession." Xin-Lao's eyes were bright. They had been on this train for a while and were eager for another passenger.

CAPITOL HILL

After drinks, they walked through Capitol Hill past dozens and dozens of hip storefronts. The shops sold mason-jar six-packs of chia pudding; instant micro-knit custom socks, home goods reconstituted from previous-century architectural salvage, t-shirts woven from bottles pulled from the Pacific garbage patch, solar oven-roasted chocolate, haptic sex suits, and more. Each store was focused and niche, catering not to an individual person but an individual whim or passing interest. In uber-liberal Seattle, shops sold things like candles that somehow repopulated the world with honeybees. In the Middle States, the wares would be equally diverse and targeted, but with an Uncle Bo's Fly-Fishing vibe about them. Each thematic direction emerged from the same gaping maw of algorithmically generated ideas.

The era of the franchise had long since passed. The world had abandoned shopping centers and chain restaurants, lurching toward small businesses to fill those gaps. And in the wake of that lurch the ad agencies had surfed in. They started by branding the ideas of small business owners, then slipped into selling business ideas along with the branding. With the amount of data algorithms were pulling to brand the latest Crotzle, it was a small step to simply suggesting the right location for said Crotzle to be sold. Now with mixed reality ad data to predict market viability with scary accuracy, it was easy for a person to go buy a generative small business idea, complete with the manufacturing, supply chain, and branding baked in. With all that in place, loans had become automated into the process and the world was growing perfectly curated shops and cafes like a thin layer of mold. They stepped into a store selling kimono-style tops. Hanna circled back to the conversation in the restaurant.

"I'm not sure I follow you. Are you saying that we've lost our excitement for new ideas?"

"Did people really used to feel that kind of excitement? I guess I thought that was just a caricature portrayed in anime." Hanna was trying on a black kimono top and was wondering what people used to put in the sleeve pockets. Keys? Change? Back when those things still existed outside of kitsch collectible shops...

"That looks really good on you." Xin-Lao flicked the feed from their eyes into Hanna's so she could see the way she looked. It always felt off, seeing herself as someone else did rather than the reversed image from a mirror. Hanna shook Xin-Lao's feed out of her view and saw Xin-Lao appraising her in a way Hanna hadn't expected. The haptics in the kimono created a feedback loop from her flushed cheeks. Hanna's OS rightly predicted her hesitation and turned the sensation down, dulling the butterflies in her stomach.

"Thanks," Hanna replied, taking off the kimono top and blinking a picture of the tag.

"People really did feel that way," Xin-Lao said.

They carried on shopping and talking about Xin-Lao's idea that the entire human race was adrift in a sea of hyper-curated, overly targeted desire. That everyone was experiencing a kind of overstimulation leading to liking lots of things but never truly loving anything.

The car they called was a generic autonomous carriage with benches facing one another. As they stepped in, Hanna's OS predicted correctly that she wanted to go home. Presumably, Xin-Lao's did the same. They slid silently into motion.

Hanna absentmindedly bought the kimono top, imagining the Amazon Fulfilment Drone that was beating her home to drop it off at the package center on the roof of her building.

Xin-Lao smiled at her. "You bought it, didn't you?"

"Yeah, just now."

"But why did you buy it?"

"Just seemed like the thing to do, I guess."

"One of my partners is putting on an art exhibit. I want you to go check it out," Xin-Lao said.

"Sounds great. Where and when?"

"I'll send you the details."

Hanna stepped from the car, looking back over her shoulder. Xin-Lao smiled at her unreservedly as the car pulled away. They looked like the embodiment of OTAKU. A beacon of unabashed enthusiasm in a sea of curated pleasantness.

EAST LAKE

As Hanna walked up to her building's elevator bank, her OS notified her about the kimono top waiting in her mail cubby. She opted to leave it, knowing it could sit there safely for days. What had it been like when there was enough anonymity in the world to allow for theft?

On her way up, her mind wandered to the look Xin-Lao had given her in the shop and her face flushed again. Calling up her contacts list, she filtered for past sexual partners, glancing at the colored rings surrounding their profile pictures denoting availability. She selected Rex (whose parents had named him Tyrannosaurus, forcing him to adopt his middle name) and changed her own status indicator to invitation. By the time she was taking off her boots, he was on his way over.

Hanna walked into her closet, struggling to reach the top of the zipper on her dress. She took it off and dropped it to the floor and into a pile of discarded clothing she had instructed her tidy bot to leave alone. The remainder of her outfit went in the laundry hamper, and she slipped into the shower. Stepping out and drying off, her OS informed her of Rex's ETA. He was only a few minutes out, so she threw an oversized sweater over her naked body. Then, feeling a chill, she added a pair of thick-knit thigh-high socks—the slight gap of skin they left exposed under the hemline of her sweater left her with a hint of excitement, a mild exhibitionism.

The door opened. Rex was tall and wiry, a typical Capitol Hill cafe-dweller dressed in black. He was a devotee of punk rock bands from the 1980s, but Hanna doubted he understood much about the culture those bands fought to carve out for themselves. Somehow his hair always looked like he'd just dried it with a towel after walking in from the rain. She took his coat, throwing it over a chair at her dining table, and ushered him into the living room.

"How's your day been?" Rex asked from her couch.

"A little odd, to be honest. I was hoping you might help with distraction." Hanna changed her status indicator to the magenta used to indicate consent. He seemed surprised or even disappointed at the lack of conversation. Still, it didn't take long for that to pass, and he was standing, pulling her into his body, hands sliding up and inside her bulky sweater.

They fell back onto the couch and Hanna guided his hands, one between her legs, one up to her throat. He followed her lead, gripping her there but with a pressure that was only for show. Hanna pulled him toward her, her own hand on his forearm, encouraging. She could feel his hesitation. Rex, always the accommodating lover, did eventually get into it. He became more forceful, clearer in his own lustful intentions. Hanna began to let herself go into the experience, loving the paradoxical feeling of control she found in giving herself up to someone else.

He was on top of her. Revealing her naked body from under her sweater, he let go of her throat to remove his belt. Before he could toss it aside, Hanna took it from him, laying it suggestively across her neck. Taking the hint Rex collared her, the feeling of the leather tightening made her wet. He pulled her close. She could feel his breath on her ear.

"Take me," Hanna said, and she blinked to turn off the information flowing between them. Rex stopped abruptly.

"Whoa, hey. What are you doing?" he said, yanking her out of the moment.

"Really? You won't fuck me without a data overlay?"

"I mean, that's risky at the best of times. But how can we both feel safe doing *this* without consent indicators?" He straightened up, holding the end of the belt to drive home his concern.

"Where's the fear of going too far?" Hanna pushed him off in frustration. He was visibly hurt. She pulled his belt from her throat and tossed it at him. "You should probably go. I'll grab you a car."

As she ushered him out the door, she gave him a thin smile and a peck on the cheek. "Whatever happened to using a safe word?" she said, mostly to herself.

"A what?" Rex replied through the closing door.

Hanna slumped onto her couch and changed her status back to public. A message came in. Xin-Lao's voice spoke through the audio system in her home.

"I'm going to launch an event company. I need you to do the branding. No algos. Design it yourself. We'll call the company OTAKU." Their recorded voice was inviting. There was no demand in it, only a tone of infectious excitement.

Hanna stood, walked over to her fridge, and pulled out some leftover yakisoba. Absentmindedly eating it over the sink, she thought about the message. She hadn't designed a logo since school. It was something they forced you to do in your first year as an academic hazing. Even the teachers admitted how impractical it was, given the reality of working in design.

Hanna did, in fact, still own a pencil and some paper. She was only a few years out of school, having started later than most, so there was a box somewhere with supplies. She called up the cube index from her building's storage, glanced over the contents of each box, and said a box number to her OS with a mouth full of noodles. As she tossed the container into the compost hatch there was a chime at the door. Waiting outside was a storage cube. She picked it up by its handles and its small-wheeled base scooted off, returning to the bowels of the building.

With sketchbook in hand, Hanna faced something she hadn't seen in her entire career—a blank page. There was a wash of fear. Where do ideas come from?

"It's okay," she reminded herself. "If it's shit, you don't have to show anyone. Ever."

She started playing around with cute cat faces but immediately felt like it was overly referential. So obviously Japanese. Pages of poorly formed ideas and obvious choices hit the floor in crumpled balls. The four-legged tidy bot kept darting out from its hidey-hole across the bamboo flooring to pick them up. This was more paper than Hanna had ever used at one time. At least she'd see a credit on her waste bill from all the recycling. The process felt gluttonous and reminded her that she'd never been all that good at drawing.

She became convinced that iconography was a dead end and started exploring a simple play on type. The ideas began as complex, hand-drawn lettering. Ribbon-style cursive, letters made from negative space, other effort-laden designs that felt full of themselves. As things became simpler and simpler, her confidence grew.

Stripping away element after element, she was slowly able to disavow herself of what she was paid to do at work. Stop thinking about what people will respond to. Make something you're excited about. It was too simple in the end, and she started cursing herself. The evening's events bubbled over, her sexual frustration with Rex somehow busting into her creative process. That overly respectful phony, listening to the Dead Kennedys without a clue what their music was actually about. It threw her down a rabbit hole remembering her dad playing 1980s punk rock for her while showing her a box of her grandfather's things. She remembered him pulling a pair of cardboard glasses from that box and placing them on her face—those ancient 3D glasses with one red and one cyan lens.

Her OS used her lenses to grab the hand-drawn lettering in her sketchbook and drag it into a design app she kept around for work. With a change she was able to modify the lettering and there it was. The idea had snuck in, without her consent.

MOSHI MOSHI CREATIVE

It felt silly walking into the Moshi Moshi office the next morning with a folder under her arm. She had tracked down a place to print her logo, but no one carried anything in their office, least of all a creative idea on paper. Hanna made her way to the desks her team was occupying that day and set the folder down before leaning back to let the morning's messages flood her field of vision. Client issues, managerial ineptitude. She was in awe of the kinds of people who made their way into management positions and how they seemed to know next to nothing about marketing. Agency life was better than big tech in this respect but only marginally.

She sat back, boots on the desk, face tilted up at the ceiling, reading message after message that had come in overnight. It seemed the Asia office had presented a Japanese client with yesterday's round of logo options and one of the designs evoked a truly offensive kanji. The account people were leaning into a hurricane-level shitstorm and her boss was ready to put the engineering team up against the wall. It was shocking to everyone that the company's algo hadn't caught it. There were checks and balances in place to avoid this exact issue.

Hanna felt something on her calf. Pulling her focus away from the message thread, she saw Mason standing there with a hand on her leg. He stood by the desk, well inside her personal space, running his eyes along the sculpted lines of her leggings. Hanna sat there stunned for a moment before she could think to flash a lack of consent. His gaze made its way up to her face, clearly registering the signal. Considering it, he smiled thinly before removing his hand. There was an overt violation in the pause, one so outside the bounds of custom it was unthinkable. Breaking free from the moment, Hanna jerked her legs from the desk, bumping him slightly in the process.

"Sorry," she said.

"That's fine," Mason replied, still standing too close.

"What's up?"

"You said you'd go for that drink with me this week."

"Actually, I said I was busy when you asked me last week. That's not the same thing." Hanna stood, gathering her folder from the desk.

Mason turned his eyes on the folder. "What's that then?"

"Nothing. Side project."

"I'm not going to stop asking." He closed what little space there was between them as he spoke. Then, looking her right in the eyes, seemingly right through her lack of consent, he went on. "You'll come around, love."

He walked away, leaving her shaken.

The day went on and Hanna shoved the experience out of mind, unable to file it properly. Work ended up being a full day of damage control. Her team didn't have a lot to do as the engineers tore apart the algo to see what had happened.

Mason led a team of those engineers, so she found herself in a few meetings with him. He barely acknowledged her.

As things wound down for the day, Hanna was working in the design lounge and Xin-Lao walked in. They were wearing their usual oversized coat. This time it played a strange mashup of ancient black and white cinema with scenes that never took place—obviously deep fakes. Hanna had on the kimono top from their shopping jaunt and a pair of high-laced, black cactus leather combat boots. Xin-Lao walked over, appraising her whole look, smiling.

"You look nice," they said.

"Thanks," Hanna said. Her cheeks flushed. Her OS didn't turn it down this time.

"How was your evening after we split? Did you get my message last night?"

"It was okay. A failed booty call if I'm being honest. And yes, I pulled a pencil and paper out of storage."

"I want to hear about both of those things!" Xin-Lao clapped their hands excitedly in a way that seemed oddly childish for someone so refined. It was cute, Hanna decided after a moment. "Want to do dinner? We can meet at a new place my OS recommended."

The two of them started towards the building's exit.

"Sure, sounds great. Just pass the location along." As Hanna said this, she noticed Mason also leaving that way. She froze, stomach turning.

"Hold on. You, okay?" Xin-Lao spun and placed themself right in Hanna's path, stopping her.

"It's okay... it's nothing."

"Doesn't look like nothing."

"Actually, would you be up for walking together?" Hanna asked.

"Sure thing. Just need to go home to charge my coat," Xin-Lao replied.

"I don't want to intrude."

"What?" Xin-Lao looked at her with confusion. "Come to my home, you odd woman. It will be fun to introduce you to my partners. They'll dig you, for sure."

"Okay, let's go." They left the office in lockstep, Hanna's folder of paper under one arm.

CHERRY HILL

Xin-Lao's place was in a renovated discount grocery store in Cherry Hill. As the car dropped them off, Hanna saw the faded Grocery Outlet sign had been changed to read Sorcery Outlet Lofts. Xin-Lao shared the live/work studio with two men. The three of whom flocked from bedroom to bedroom like migratory birds—Xin-Lao's words.

"You two will eat here," Earl said.

Earl stood across the kitchen island smiling at the two of them. He was a slab of a man with shoulders wider than the hallways of Hanna's micro apartment.

"I don't want to put you out at all," Hanna said.

Earl laughed and reached for Xin-Lao as they rounded the island. "Who is this you've brought home, Lao?" Xin-Lao rose on tippy toes and kissed him, their hand on his chin to coax him lower. Earl's mountain of a body encompassed their slight frame. They kissed like they were savoring each other, nothing like the perfunctory pecks or the hungry mauling Hanna had in her toolkit. It was easy between the two of them and flauntingly sensual.

"I was hoping for some time alone with my friend, hon," Xin-Lao teased, looking back at Hanna.

"That sounds perfect," Earl replied. "You two will have all the space you need. What would you like to eat?"

"Surprise us. I need to go hang my coat on the charger." Xin-Lao turned toward a room in the back, stepping out of their oversized garment sculpture. They were wearing surprisingly little under it. Hanna found herself staring at their petite frame, wrapped in nothing but some tightfitting undergarments.

Earl was taking in Hanna's reaction and chuckling. "They call it their coat of armor."

Hanna pulled herself together. "So, how long have you two been partnered up?" Hanna asked Earl as he threw a tent-sized apron over his chest.

"Couple years, I think. I came on the scene as the third. Lao has been in love with Yevgeny for a lot longer. I met the two of them when they were still casual, just orbiting each other. Hooking up and collaborating on various art projects. I like to think I was the stabilizing force that made it possible for them to live together."

"Sounds like there's a real spark between the two of them."

"Yeah, it's a beautiful thing to witness. Two people who burn too bright to make it as a couple." The large man's face was genuine, with a half-smile. It drew Hanna in. He started pulling ingredients from the fridge and manipulating them expertly with a chef's knife. Hanna took it as her cue to wander.

The main living area was cavernous. Artifacts of early-century retail still left faint impressions. Holes in the concrete where shelving had hung, silver conduit snaking along the ceiling. There was a large frame mounted to the wall housing a tapestry, its fine threads combining to form an intricate, abstract pattern. As Hanna looked at it, her lenses zoomed in to focus on a tiny loom node no more than a millimeter wide. The weaving bot raced across the threads with hair-like legs trailing behind it. It was completing the tapestry. Her eye then caught another glimpse of movement on the far side of the tapestry. Zooming in again, Hanna could see a second bot racing frantically to undo the first one's work. It was pulling apart the woven thread as it worked, trying to undo the whole thing from the other end.

"It's an old adversarial neural network from the early machine-learning days." Xin-Lao was behind her, still wearing next to nothing.

"And you've trapped it in a tapestry?"

"Yevgeny found the code in some historian's collection. We worked together to train one of the algos on a wide set of abstract art. Algo A has been winning for about a month. That is why there's something to see in the frame. I think we're coming up on a dismantling period. You're lucky. There's rarely a full tapestry."

"I have always had good timing."

"That's an attractive quality."

Hanna and Xin-Lao ate a thali Earl had assembled at the kitchen island, a half dozen small, silver bowls of Indian flavors for them to moan over.

"So, let's see it," Xin-Lao said, pushing aside the dishes to make space for the paper folder.

"I don't know now. I'm not sure I want to show you such a half-baked idea. It's so far outside the bounds of acceptable design these days. It's overly simple and referential to a seriously out-of-style period. I know you wanted something an algo wouldn't come up with, but there's reasoning behind their design parameters." Hanna tried to soften the inevitable rejection.

She opened the folder and the two of them stared at it in silence for a moment.

"This is everything," Xin-Lao said, almost in a whisper. Then they turned toward Hanna and leaned in, pausing right before their lips touched. Their breath warm and fragrant from dinner. The kiss was a sudden low-pressure system, a monsoon.

SOUTHCENTER MALL

She stepped out of the driverless Lyft and into a dark parking lot. Hanna had seen the old abandoned Southcenter Mall before but only from the freeway on the way out to the airport. From a distance, it looked like a lost city with its mysterious dark structures overrun by morning glory and blackberries. What must have once been decorative trees now dwarfed burned out lamp posts, and cracked concrete gave way to long grass.

Up close it was dirty. She stood among trash and debris left by generations of unhoused people. People whose existence was still unacknowledged by the Pacific States, a nation loudly claiming to have no homeless citizens. She watched a little wistfully as her car retreated back to the freeway. It had taken her as far into the abandoned mall as it was willing, leaving her to walk the rest of the way. Hanna wore an ankle-length dark green coat and she pulled it around her body to shield herself from the light rain. Under her protective outer layer, her body was hugged in a black, form-fitting dress. It was sleeveless and had a hemline that stopped midcalf, leaving a small space between it and her hightops. The coat was made from a waxy material that reminded her of a tarp. Rain beaded and rolled down it like condensation on a glass.

Hanna had never set foot in a mall before. It seemed to take forever to get to an entrance. The amount of real estate dedicated to parking was just crazy. There was something backward about getting in a car to go shop only to drive your purchase home with you. The pin Xin-Lao had sent her earlier that day led her into a small side door of a giant building and down a long corridor. The hallway opened up into the second floor of a courtyard. Down below metal picnic tables circled a dry fountain. The space was ringed with little storefronts, signage intact, selling food from around the world.

There were people wandering the atrium below and others perched along the edge of the upper level. As she joined them a notification hit her.

You came to see this. Agree to installation? Which she did. And there it was, seemingly out of the blue, the OTAKU logo floating above the rusted courtyard, its lettering always facing her as she made her way down the motionless escalator that led into a thin crowd below. People were milling about down there, walking in small groups, letting out murmurs of wonder.

Hanna's coat brushed the sides of the escalator as she walked down, making a noise as she went. She found a picnic table to sit on. As her hightops hit the bench, she started to see thin wisps of particles tracing behind people as they walked. So thin at first that she thought it was dust kicked up from the floor. Then, as the moments passed, the wisps blossomed into plumes and started to take on colors. They billowed out of people's faces and erupted in spurts off their wrists and ankles, eddying behind them as they moved. Before long, everyone was walking through each other's clouds and the colors began to swirl and mix. It was like a school of cephalopods trailing ink plumes. Or an enormously complex data visualization depicting God knows what.

The plumes were fluid and complex. It was mesmerizing. As the clouds began to fill the space,

Hanna could only tell where someone was by searching for the focal point of their movement, the spigot from which their data flowed. People's conversations floated through the colorful clouds. There were tones of unbridled excitement. Everyone was talking about how they had heard about the exhibit, who they suspected was behind it, and when the next one might be.

"Fuck me. I think they pulled it off," Hanna said to herself.

One of the nexus points moving through the plumes came toward her and a person emerged. The man was scarecrow-like. His face was angular, led by a beak of a nose. Black skinny jeans hugged his narrow legs and the black blazer he wore was made from some kind of unusual fabric that was too stiff and hung like crumpled wax paper. One side of his blazer collar was absentmindedly popped up. He looked over at her and nodded but said nothing. The way he gazed at the spectacle with clinical curiosity, rather than wonder, led Hanna to realize it was Yevgeny.

"It's a representation of personal data being emitted. I get that much," Hanna said.

"It's not a representation. It's live. That's the actual data people are emitting," Yevgeny replied.

"I'm sorry, what?"

He turned to look back at her as he spoke. "This is the live data stream Alphabet pulls off every person. Biometrics, semantic search history, online activity across every media channel—the works. I just made it pretty."

"That's impossible. You're telling me you got your hands on the Alphabet learning algo and managed to train it to re-enact this? You could never get a dataset large enough to teach it with."

"This isn't their learning algo trained on mocked up data, I'm using the real thing," he said matter-of-factly.

Hanna stopped in her mental tracks, unable to reconcile that idea. The value in an algo was the training data it had to work with. The Alphabet algo was what it was because of the information it had been fed over the last century. To steal the code was one thing, but to somehow get your hands on their full, working algo...

Every major company on Earth used the Alphabet algo to power their work. Moshi Moshi depended on it to drive their ideation process. But it was a black box they weren't allowed to look into, let alone fuck around with.

"That would be the greatest intellectual property theft in human history."

"Can it really be called theft?" He smiled. "This is art."

"I call bullshit," Hanna said, rejecting the ideal wholesale. "You expect me to believe that you stole the technology that underpins the global economy? And that you're making art projects with it in abandoned shopping centers? And that you did it without the powers that be finding out?"

"Believe what you like," Yevgeney replied.

MOSHI MOSHI BOARDROOM

The team of engineers offered little in the way of explanation in the meeting about the logo fuckup from the day before. It seemed as though the lapse in Moshi Moshi's design process couldn't be tied back to anything internal. They had gone over the company code line by line, and it was behaving perfectly. The only thing they could suggest was unthinkable—that somehow there had been an issue with the Alphabet algo it depended on.

Mason was defending his team against some executive Hanna had never seen before. "Look, we've QA'd this thing a dozen times. There's nothing wrong with it."

"Well that seems to fly in the face of the fucking account we just lost now, doesn't it?" The exec-man said. He was handsome, in his early fifties, and wore a very expensive blazer over a t-shirt and jeans. He was also wearing glasses, something Hanna hadn't seen anyone do in years.

"There was a moment when the Alphabet algo dropped offline. Three-tenths of a second. I'm telling you that's the only thing we found," Mason said.

"Saying there was corrupt data is absurd. It's never happened. Not in the history of this company or any other," exec-man said.

"It wasn't corrupt data. I'm saying the algo was just gone for a fraction of a second."

As the meeting room emptied, Hanna brushed by Mason. He didn't even look at her, which confirmed the gravity of things in a way nothing else could. Heads were rolling in IT.

It was a day of back-to-back meetings. The next was with a client the firm had been courting for months, the Nunavut Water Counsel. The NWC, or Big Water as most people called it, was a private corporation founded by the Inuit and other First

Nations in Northern Canada. Having won significant legal battles disputing freshwater rights up there, they had formed a legal entity over fifty years ago and built a powerful business out of the world's most valuable resource.

From what Hanna remembered of her North American history playlists in school, a number of events in the late 20s had swung Canada into prosperity and prominence on the world stage. An established pandemic response, a commitment to blockchain tech in government, early adoption of a universal basic income, and liberal immigration policies came together in a perfect storm of financial success. At the same time China had begun shutting itself off from the world, Russia began engaging Eastern Europe in decades of incremental wars, and the United States fractured leaving room on the global stage for a new economic power. One fueled largely by access to potable water.

Mr. Aput and a few key people from the NWC sat across the table from Hanna, Xin-Lao, and a couple other people from her team. Between them stood a set of miniature monolithic sculptures, each looking like a stylized angular stone pillar. They were a water packaging concept inspired by the legs of Inukshuk and felt a little on the nose in the wake of this recent cultural insensitivity scandal at Moshi Moshi. Hanna looked at them nervously with nothing left to do but swing at the pitch in front of her.

"Since the target market for these is the Southwestern States and parts of Texas, we went with this rockwork idea. The feeling is that the aesthetic will appeal to that market, while still offering a cultural nod to you. For obvious reasons the name choices will be hyper-local, most likely referring to lost water sources in the areas they're sold into." Hanna paused to read the room, watching for signs of appropriation outrage. With her faith in the company's design output shaken, this job was a lot harder.

"It's a fun play. I can appreciate the work that has gone into this idea." Mr. Aput spoke with the intonation of old wealth, even though his people had come to it within a generation. There was a calm about him, as if he had been waiting patiently for his return to power for hundreds of years.

"That's great to hear," Hanna said, feeling the mood in the room lighten.

Then the woman to Mr. Aput's right spoke up. Hanna's OS reminded her that the woman's name was Tapeesa.

"I don't see how it will work for our supply chain. We primarily use slow airships, and space is always an issue on those blimps." She was young, around Hanna's age, and striking. Her jet-black hair was pulled into two braids that fell past her shoulders.

Now it was the team's time to shine. Xin-Lao had pushed hard for a packing parameter on the design inputs during this project, so it was their job to do the big reveal. Without speaking, they stood and began assembling the water cartons. There were nine of them on the table and they fit together like a puzzle to form a perfect cube. It was the kind of baller move that won business.

Meeting bled into meeting and the day finally resolved. Hanna was halfway down the building's walkway to the street when she felt a hand on the small of her back.

Mason's voice was right in her ear accompanied by the smell of stale breath. "What a total clusterfuck. Makes me want to get messy drunk and let off some steam. You know the feeling?"

Hanna pulled away, but his hand slid firmly around her waist. She turned to face him, unable to believe what was happening. He stepped toward her, forcing her back against the railing of the covered walkway, one hand still on her waist.

"What are you doing?" Her haptics were going haywire, her OS unable to account for the way she was feeling.

"Playing hard to get is so out of style, sweetheart." His hand began to drift down. "You like multiple partners? What's one more?"

"I'm... I'm sorry. I have plans," Hanna stammered. She broke free of him and speed-walked down the walkway to a waiting car. On the ride home, she started to kick herself. How could that be her reaction to assault? Replaying the scene in her mind, there were so many ways to stand up to him. She was furious with herself. Tears streamed down her cheeks.

Arriving home, Hanna turned off her status indicator and went dark. She stood in the shower until she could no longer taste salt running down her cheeks, unable to understand why she had apologized again.

PIONEER SQUARE TUNNEL

anna lay in bed naked after her shower. Without the haptic clothing to modulate her feelings, she cycled through rapid waves of anger and embarrassment. Eventually, she told her OS to flip her status public. Along with the usual work chat, she found a video message from Xin-Lao. They were standing at the end of an old tunnel with brick archways. The structure was shored up by aluminum I-beams and diffused purple light waved across their face from an unseen source above them.

"We're missing you tonight," Xin-Lao said. The camera view rotated away from a piece of mirror mounted on the wall they were using to record the message and Hanna could see the tunnel more clearly. People walked its length and milled about in silence. No doubt another art exhibit, only perceived by those in attendance.

Xin-Lao rotated the full 360 and facing the mirror again, blew Hanna a kiss. The video feed cut out, followed by a location notification. The last thing Hanna wanted to do was go anywhere. She had planned on eating in bed and watching a VR livestream of some shitty border crime show.

In spite of herself, she dragged her ass up and threw on some slim-fitting combat gear she curated last fall—tight, black Lycra denim pants with a tank top, draped in an oversized black army jacket with too many pockets, a brimmed army surplus cap, a kaffiyeh around the neck, and black combat boots on her feet. Her OS dialed in her haptics to guarded.

The location was on the waterfront up against the submerged neighborhood of Pioneer Square. Feeling unfit for public interaction, Hanna chose the most expensive way to get there. Taking the elevator to the roof, she had her OS call an AirLyft. The two-seat drone was already waiting on its pad when she arrived. She climbed in and the safety mechanisms engaged as the glass door thunked closed. The flight from her place in Eastlake to the far edge of downtown took no time at all. She passed right over the Space Needle, a monument built well over a century ago, every line of its design screaming of a vision for the future that Hanna lived in now. They got so many things wrong. On the other hand, she was flying over it in an airborne taxi, so what did she know?

Hanna touched down on a rooftop near the location Xin-Lao had shared. After taking the elevator down she stepped out onto the street. She stopped in her tracks when she saw the OTAKU logo flashing in front of her. There was a staircase descending below street level, the kind of thing she would have walked by her whole life if it weren't for the mixed reality sign hanging above it.

She stepped down the stairs, through an open metal door, and found a deserted passage. It led her through a series of turns and the architecture grew older as she walked. By the time she found the crowd things were positively historic, and she had no doubt that she was underwater. Her OS was prompted with the same notification from the mall. *You came to see this. Agree to installation?*

Hanna agreed, and a faint hum seeped into her skull through the bone induction speakers woven into her hat and tank top. It started so softly that she imagined it was white noise coming from the ocean overhead. Then it grew, folding in on itself to form a beat. It was a subtle, down-tempo thing. Just the foundation of a composition. Not music. Not yet at least. There were considerably more people here than Yevgeny's first one at the mall. Xin-Lao's mission to drive people to a level of obsession that had been lost to history must have been working.

As she made her way into the thin crowd, the composition she was hearing began to pick up notes from people around her. It was pulling fragments of the data they emitted as she passed, converting it into musical elements and layering pieces of their experiences on top of her own. She found herself walking through an orchestra, each person's contribution to her audio coming and going as they passed. The ones walking alongside her harmonizing and weaving with her composition, others passing in and out with moments of dissonance. It always threatened to become melodic but stayed just out of reach. The effect was deeply moving, and Hanna found that it stirred up the day's experiences in her, resurfacing feelings she was fighting to pave over. Tears streamed silently down her cheeks.

A hand brushed the small of her back and Hanna spun violently. "Don't fucking touch me!" she spat.

Xin-Lao stood there, hands raised, palms forward. The people around them looked over, surprised at the interruption. Yevgeny was a couple of paces behind, and Xin-Lao waved him off without looking back. Closing the gap between them they looked into Hanna's wet eyes and moved in for a hug.

=

The three of them sat at an ancient wooden table in front of an old storefront. They seemed to be in a tunnel that lay below a sidewalk. It was totally disorienting.

Yevgeny started to explain. "Back a couple of centuries ago, what used to be downtown Seattle burned to the ground. So, they rebuilt, but everything got all fucked up with the city rebuilding the streets and shop owners rebuilding sidewalks and buildings. By the time it was all said and done the storefronts were lower than street level, so they needed to be covered up. These tunnels have been below the sidewalks of Pioneer Square ever since. Now the whole neighborhood is underwater. Some friends of mine have been down here, pumping out the water and pressurizing tunnels. It's some kind of venture capital-backed experiment. They want to see if anyone will rent office space under the ocean."

"That's a lot to take in," Hanna said.

"Yeah, give her a moment to collect herself before you go off like that," teased Xin-Lao.

"That was a trauma reaction when Lao touched you." Yevgeny said.

"I've had a tough day," Hanna said. "Listen, I can't believe I'm saying this... Did you two really manage to steal the Alphabet Algo off of the Moshi Moshi cloud?"

"You told me it would be untraceable." Xin-Lao's tone was low and angry. "Also, are you just walking about telling people? Clearly I trust Hanna, but how could you know that?"

"You said you wanted her in, so I told her the truth." He said, then looking at Hannah. "Sorry to speak about you as though you're not here." Looking back at Xin-Lao "The chances of it interfering with the agency's work was a statistical anomaly." Yevgeny didn't seem phased by being caught in the act of a crime that would... Actually, Hanna had no idea at all what would happen. It was an act of literally unthinkable theft.

Yevgeny answered her unasked question. "If anyone finds out, Alphabet will have Pacific States Border Security throw us down a dark hole."

"Hey, isn't that Tapeesa from our meeting today with Big Water?" Hanna said, nodding in the direction of a First Nations woman across the way. The woman looked at them for a moment, then walked into the stream of people and disappeared.

The conversation they'd had, paired with the appearance of Tapeesa put an uneasy note on an already uneasy evening for Hanna. Something about seeing the woman from Big Water there brought the reality of what was going on sharply into focus, making her believe in the algo theft. She didn't last much longer at the exhibit.

VACTUBE

The vactube rail network spread through the major cities of Washington, Oregon, and Northern California, with newer lines terminating in Boise and Vancouver. The Pacific States established free travel and trade with one another right after the States Rights Split and now an agreement was developing between Washington and Iowa.

Hanna read the morning's feed. The back of the seat in front of her had a featureless surface for her OS to project text and images on. She preferred to read the day's news rather than listen to it. Each subject group scrolled up as she read, moving with her gaze.

OTAKU. The word hit her like a truck. There was a review of Xin-Lao and Yevgeny's exhibit by one of the most followed culture curators in Seattle. It described the generative music installation in such detail that it stirred up feelings from the night before. The thought of this kind of exposure was alarming.

Sensing her reaction, her OS requested more information. It ran a full semantic search, creating a dashboard of all mentions. The story's reach was hard to believe. While there were a handful of first-hand accounts from attendees, the bulk of the chatter seemed to be people trying to track down the creators. Speculation was spreading not only about the artist or artists but also about the statement made by the work.

She found a SubReddit dissecting the branding. Heated arguments were taking place about the design parameters needed to generate something so outside the norm. Someone suggested it must be human-designed, only to be shouted down for being a conspiracy theorist.

Hanna pushed her OS to search further, probing the network that was growing around the event, digging for any connections between it and Yevgeny's unthinkable theft, but no one was walking that path. She pulled away and forced herself into work.

She was on a run to Reno, gathering local intel for the regional branding of the packaged water design they'd pitched to the Nunavut Water Group. When branding products to sell outside of the Pacific States, the team often had to physically go there to get naming information. The info coming out of places like Nevada, Arizona, and Utah was too fucked to make sense of. If you wanted to name something after a lost water source, as she did now, there was no guarantee that what you could find online would be true.

A conspiracy theory had been recycled in Nevada last year and some of the crazier locals got it in their heads that the contrails left by large aircraft were brainwashing them or something. As a result, interstate flights had been grounded due to shoulder-mounted rocket scares around airports. Now the best way to get to Reno was a vactube to the Bay Area, then a drive across state lines with a local fixer. The whole thing seemed wildly impractical to Hanna, but that was the job sometimes.

As the three-hour journey came to an end, a video message popped up in her lenses. Seeing it was from Mason, Hanna flicked it off to the side. He'd never sent her anything directly before, and it turned her stomach. Then, realizing that she was going to need to take care of this growing problem, she played it.

Mason was recording in the window of some storefront, looking into his reflection as he spoke. Something was wrong. He looked haggard. Actually, he looked scared.

"What the fuck did you and your little friends do? I know you've been hanging around with that tiny girl in the giant coat, but... fuck, Hanna. What's happening? It's not possible. There's no way you could have stolen it. Listen, I don't know what you've gotten yourself into, but now you have to give it to me or they will... I don't know. They're threatening to tell my family things. Things I've never told anyone, cognito data that only my OS has seen. Fuck! Just give me the algo." He looked away at something, then cut the feed.

Hanna was in complete shock, but not so much so that she missed the intentional misgendering of her friend. The train came to a stop at North Beach Station. Hanna shut down her work channels and stood to disembark. Just ahead of her she saw a familiar set of braids. Straining to look through the crowd, she thought she caught a glimpse of

Tapeesa's face again. By the time Hanna stood on the platform the woman was gone.

It was midday, meaning the only way to get anywhere in San Francisco was on a mobility wheel. Single wheels with foot pegs on either side so that you rode them like unicycles without seats. Walking over to a charging bay one rolled over to her and she hopped on giving it directions to her hotel. Her OS set the driving preferences to fast and loose, then adjusted her clothing to become rigid in certain areas to support her body as the wheel accelerated into traffic. It flew, mostly sticking to the bike lanes, but occasionally whipping in and out of traffic. Her clothing spoke to it, propping her up as it cornered, hugging her hamstrings and back with the acceleration. She zoned out, letting her haptics respond to the ride so she could think.

Mason, for all of his glaring faults, was a solid dev. He was as likely as anyone she knew to understand the tech behind a personal OS. That his cognito data had been breached was surprising. That he took part in shady activities that could be used against him, not so much. Still, the fundamental promise of a personal OS was encryption. Even though Hanna was developing a strong urge to kick the shit out of him, she'd be shocked if he didn't know how to hide his online activity. Someone was blackmailing him with the semantic history he kept private—something that shouldn't be possible.

What had her own activity looked like recently? The use of one's OS was so embedded, being hacked like that would be like having your mind read. She suddenly remembered her OS looking for connections between the last OTAKU exhibit and Yevgeny and her stomach leaped into her throat. Hannah spent the rest of the ride unable to focus, thinking about the fate of her friends. Fretting about the possibility that she may have exposed them further.

SOMA HOTEL

The wheel dropped her off at her hotel in the SoMa district. Paid for by her work, this room would be a step up from the kind of coffin stacks she rented on her own dime. Hanna walked to the elevator as her OS checked her in. First, excitement when she learned the room had a shower, then less so when the elevator descended to the floors below street level. The room turned out to be pretty nice. A bunk on top of a closed-in bathroom area with enough space to toss her bag on the floor by the ladder. Hanna climbed the ladder, lay back, and thought for a moment.

She pulled up a tight network of friends—people she knew would step up if she ever had a real ask. Setting up a parameter to send a message to each of their likewise trusted networks, Hanna put out a call for advice. The matchmaking system would verify a mutual connection with a blockchain key.

"I'm in San Francisco and just had a weird experience with data privacy. Looking for a friend of a friend in the area with expertise in OS encryption. Given the subject matter, it might be best to meet in person. Any takers? I pay in beer." Flipping off the broadcast, she sent it as a text only message with every level of encryption she knew, hoping to come across as someone you could trust to have this conversation with.

The anonymous reply came quickly. "What's up? Any friend of a friend is a friend of mine. Let's grab that beer after a walk along the seawall." The message blinked out, replaced by a location and an ETA.

Hanna threw her coat back on, mindful of the various microclimates in San Francisco, and hit the street.

She could be at the location in minutes on a wheel but decided to prolong the journey and walk. That would get her there at the same time as her anonymous date. She pondered who the connection might be and what this person was going to look like. A ploy to distract her from the sinking gravity of her situation.

San Francisco was a gleaming, tower-filled city. The residential neighborhoods at its core had been torn down after the remote work migration of her childhood. Spurred on by the pandemic waves of the 20s, anyone who could work from home chose to. Property values nose-dove in these parts as the spending to earnings ratio of all the tech megacities collapsed in on themselves. Then it didn't take long for those people to move out of the cities, finding places where they could afford to own things. Doomsday forecasters warned that these empty metropolises would become lawless husks filled with roaming bands of copper thieves. Instead, corporate interests swept in, erecting shining, tasteless structures filled with absurdly sized data centers whose AI inhabitants were only limited by the speed of light. It was crucial that they live among their own kind to limit the tiny fractions of a second it took for them to talk with one another.

With this level of investment, San Francisco had no choice but to build the seawall. There was no amount of good money that wouldn't be thrown after bad to keep the ocean from lapping at the feet of Silicon Valley's gods. As Hanna walked along the top of that seawall, towers to the left and the bay to the right, she came upon the meeting location.

Her companion stood out. He was pudgy, something you didn't see much anymore. People still came in a variety of sizes and shapes, but the folding rolls of her parent's generation had fallen from favor in the Pacific States. A lack of animal protein, coupled with AI-enabled biometrics and haptic clothing made weight gain easy to avoid. His look was ideologically motivated. He was wearing what appeared to be hapticless clothing and a pair of painfully clunky glasses. She sat beside him and their blockchain keys chimed, signaling the mutual connection.

"Burtrum." He smiled at her, extending a hand.

She took it. "Hanna."

"Go ahead. Ask."

"Ask what, exactly?"

"You know what. Why would anyone choose to be fat while wearing these ill-fitting clothes and absurd goggles?" He chuckled as he spoke. It was disarming.

"I'm hoping it's because you're some kind of privacy nut who doesn't trust the security protocols everyone else takes as gospel."

Burtrum tapped a finger to his nose.

"Perfect, because that's who I need to hear from today," Hanna said.

"Let's walk."

EMBARCADERO

"So, I have a friend. Scratch that—I work with this asshole who claims that he's being blackmailed. He seems to be saying they grabbed something from his cognito search history. Now the idea that he is up to some shameful, extortion-level shit is totally plausible. But the other part?" Hanna shrugged.

The seawall rose up out of the old Embarcadero. As they strolled north along the top, she looked over the city-side edge. The street fell an easy two stories below them. Out of view, the other side held back the waves of the bay. From what she remembered, there had been considerable debate about how far south the seawall should be built. In the end, it stopped at SFO, the international airport. Everything south of the airport was swamped with the rising tideline and large sections of the 101 had to be elevated to save the freeway.

"Your question is whether that's possible—to steal data off of someone's OS? The short answer is yes, but it's prohibitively expensive."

"I've been living under the impression that the private interactions I have with my OS are mathematically impossible to hack. Everyone—like *everyone*—is taught that the Privacy Act of '32 led us to an encryption plateau. Our taxes fund datacenter security for fuck's sake." If Hanna hadn't asked Burtrum here, if she hadn't requested this conversation, she would have written him off as an alt-truther. Some conspiracy nut from a Middle State.

"It is possible. But if I was going to steal your data, I would need to be right next to you, like within a meter." He smiled.

"Please, don't."

"Oh, honey, I could not afford that. The tech needed to decrypt that shit is the kind of thing rogue governments rent from the NSA."

"So how does it work?"

"How's your understanding of quantum recurrent neural networks?" Burtrum asked.

"I'm a creative director at a marketing agency."

"Then maybe we'll just leave it at it's possible, but in the you-could-buy-a-city-block-with-the-money-it-takes-to-do-it way."

"Then maybe you could talk to me a little about how it's stolen, rather than how it's decrypted. Why do you need to be so close?"

"Sure. As I mentioned, the decryption is the resource intensive part. But first you need to get something to decrypt. Once that data is in a datacenter it's lost to the world. So, you need to grab it off someone as it's happening. You need to listen to it, sort of." Burtrum stopped walking and leaned his heavy torso up against the railing. They looked out at Oakland across the water. He went on. "The best I can do is a metaphor. Back in 2020, the Israeli army found a need for eavesdropping on Palestinian conversations. This was back when Gaza was still inhabitable and worth fighting over. They discovered that they could point a laser at a hanging lightbulb from some hideout across the street and an algo could decipher conversations from the slight movement of the bulb. The compression patterns in the air people made when speaking caused microscopic movements in the bulb. Not something anyone could see of course, but enough for their old AI to decipher.

"This works like that. The comparison is apt in that their spycraft only worked with a bare bulb hanging on a cord from the ceiling. The kind of data listening we're talking about works by detecting the unbelievably faint fluctuations in electrical current coming off of your skull. Your lenses use the water in our bodies as an antenna. So, grabbing the data off someone only works if the target is wearing lenses and only if the listener is close enough to get a read on the electromagnetic field from your body. Basically, within one or two meters." He stopped speaking.

Hanna stood in silence. The sun was setting behind them and the bay glowed. Huge container ships maneuvered out to sea, pushed by electric tugs under the Golden Gate Bridge. Once they reached open water, their bow cannons would launch football-field-sized parasails to carry them across the Pacific.

Hanna was trying not to think of the woman on the train. Was it possible that Tapeesa was sitting right behind her the whole ride? "If this hack is so expensive, why do you wear those dorky DIY goggles? What are the chances someone will try to steal your data?" she asked.

"What makes you think I'm not worth it?" Burtrum smiled.

NOODLE BUS

Burtrum declined Hanna's offer to take him for a beer, telling her frankly that after what she had told him he didn't want to be in a crowded space together. They had parted on friendly terms, and he gave her a one-time key to contact him again if she needed anything. The day was getting on and she still had to meet up with the fixer after dinner to talk over travel plans for the next day. She was hungry and called a noodle bus.

The one that arrived specialized in ramen. Hanna sat down at the counter and ate a bowl of stupidly good noodles. She thought about her situation as the bus drove a circuitous path timed to drop off each diner as they finished. It pulled up to her hotel. She slurped the last of the broth.

Walking into the busy hotel common area, Hanna sat on a couch and checked her feed. OTAKU was every-fucking-where. Seattle wouldn't shut up. Every major art and culture curator was talking about it, speculating about who was behind the two exhibits that had lasted one night each. Whole forums were springing up to pass along word for when the logo reappeared. People were creating little cults, offering rewards, claiming they attended the exhibits, debunking other self-proclaimed attendees, and all other manner of frothing at the mouth.

"People really were hungry for something like this," Hanna said to herself. She was about to call Xin-Lao when she stopped short, looking at all of the people sitting around her. She stood and walked to the elevator to check out the roof.

It was significantly less crowded. Finding a corner where she could be sure she had a few meters of space on every side, she pinged Xin-Lao.

Xin-Lao answered right away. "Hey, girl. How's your trip so far?"

"Pretty weird. Where are you? Are there people around?" Hanna had selected audio only.

"I'm in a bar in Georgetown. Why? What's up?"

"Like are their people within a meter of you right now?"

"Yes." Xin-Lao's tone changed with the oddness of the question.

"Can you step outside? Find somewhere with some space?"

"Hold on."

Hanna could hear her friend navigating a crowded bar, shouldering through people. The background noise changed.

"Okay. What the fuck is up?" Xin-Lao said in a whisper.

"I think Mason knows about Yevgeny's algo theft. I don't know if he's tied it to the art installations, but I can't be sure of anything. This is going to sound crazy, but it sounds like someone is blackmailing him. He says he's been hacked."

"Hang on, there's a lot to unpack here. If some shady party is after the algo that Yevgeny appropriated as an act of creative expression," Xin-Lao said in their half-mocking way, "why would they blackmail Mason? Why not go after one of us?"

"I have no idea. But you two should lie low for a bit, maybe try working from home. It's also not a great time for your plan to bring OTAKU back into people's lives," Hanna said.

"Oh, I don't know if I agree with that. Also, don't downplay the role of your branding. People are all over that aspect of the work as well." Xin-Lao's compliment made Hanna blush. She turned it down in her haptics, frustrated with the distraction.

"They're raving about the art, not the logo. Listen, I have to go but one more thing. I was just speaking with a guy down here who described a way any one of us could be hacked, but it requires that the hacker be right next to you. I know it sounds crazy, but don't assume your cognito data is private."

"Oh, that's not the only way to hack an OS," Xin-Lao said, way too casually. "Thanks, though. Good reminder. You gonna be okay?"

"Yeah, I'll be fine. This trip is only a few days. I'll be back up there and we can talk more in person. I'm not really sure what to do about Mason."

"Have you considered filing a complaint with HR?" Xin-Lao said.

Hanna was stunned. She hadn't said anything about her problems with Mason.

"It was all over your face. He's pulling shit with you, and I can see it."

Hanna stayed silent.

"Oh, fuck," said Xin-Lao. "I didn't realize it was that bad. I'm going to go boot stomp that little fucker."

Something about the way Xin-Lao said this last part surprised Hanna like they were about to drive to his house and do it. "No. Don't do anything, I'll take care of it. I'll ping you when I'm back—not sure what the comms situation is like in Nevada." Hanna ended the call.

She stood on the roof, looking west up into the hills. Why hadn't she reported the sexual harassment? Also just how dialed into this shady shit were Yevgeny and Xin-Lao. The way they had casually acknowledged other ways of hacking an OS had been weird. It left Hanna wondering what the two of them were working on for the next exhibit.

SOMA ROOFTOP

ather than picking another place to meet, Hanna shared her location with the Reno fixer and waited. The rooftop was a grassy, plant-filled park with a bar in it. People sat in small groups as the bartender deployed rolling trays laden with drinks. Hanna put in an order for a Manhattan and looked around, wondering what kind of equipment was needed to read the information subtly radiating off her skull. Her drink came and warmed the creeping chill of the San Francisco evening.

The fixer stood out starkly against the backdrop of business travelers, androgenous tech nerds, and nightlife pregamers of SoMa. The first thing Hanna noticed was his clothes. Regular haptic apparel was designed to be invisible with nanostructures woven into the fabric. This man's jacket was black with an obvious texture, the kind of ribs and lines used by the military to augment a person's movements. It ran on the same principles of biometric looping as regular clothing, but in this case, it could make someone physically impressive rather than just fine tuning their emotions. Along with the black tac jacket, he had on a pair of worn jeans, a pair of hiking boots, and a ball cap over his tousled brown hair. He was turning heads.

Hanna waved him over, which was unnecessary as his OS was no doubt telling him who she was.

"Drink?" she asked as he sat.

"Not for four years now, thanks." He smiled like he was making a dad joke.

"Clever." Hanna paused, unsure of herself. The pull to know as much as possible about this man was strong. She may be putting her life in his hands. Something stirred in her, a deep need for substantive connection she had been robbed of her whole life. The kind of thing that took time to develop. She grabbed the little case from her bag to remove her lenses. He looked surprised, then pleased. "Hanna," she said, shaking his hand.

"Jo-Jack," he replied, waiting for her reaction. It was a name that practically screamed Middle States.

"So, we're doing this blind?" he said, removing his lenses as well.

"It's a thing I'm trying. I'm tired of first impressions being all about semantic history. There's always time for that later." She decided he was handsome.

"You ever been to Nevada?" Jo-Jack asked, an accent slipping through.

"Nope, my family used to take vacations into Wyoming when I was a kid. But I haven't traveled much, other than up to Vancouver, since then. We lost that cabin back during the split. Where did you grow up to make you such an expert at interstate travel?"

"Phoenix. My family made a living moving Texans during the first wave of refugees. Then lost it all when Arizona changed the immigration laws. Our whole business was suddenly illegal." He chuckled.

"Is this trip going to be eventful? I was surprised when I was told I was going if I'm being honest," Hanna said.

"Totally routine. Do this kind of corporate work all the time. Some company like yours wants to impress a client by saying they got their intel straight from the source, so they send someone like you to talk to locals. The drive should be smooth. It's more about paying off the right people than anything else these days."

"What was it about before?"

"Not getting caught!" Jo-Jack laughed loudly, causing the few people on the rooftop who weren't already side-eyeing him to do so.

They agreed to depart early in the morning. Hanna found it hard to get a read on Jo-Jack. He straddled two stereotypes. The voice of a Southwestern alt-truther and the worldliness of a diplomat. She filed the contradiction away and returned to her room.

Lying in her bunk, she was about to veg out with a trashy VR livestream when another video message came in from Mason. With her clothes piled on the floor at the bottom of the ladder she had no way to tune down the feeling of dread. She archived the message without opening it.

HIGHWAY 80

When Jo-Jack said early, he meant 4 a.m. Hanna woke up in what she would still define as night and stood in front of the hotel. The truck that pulled up was unlike anything she had ever seen. First and foremost, it wasn't a color. It was this kind of deep, black absence of light as if someone made paint pigment from a black hole. She recognized it as vantablack, a paint made from nanotubes that reflected no light at all. You couldn't even see the angles of the metal that made up the truck cab whose door stood some four feet off the ground. The passenger door swung open, spilling light out onto the curb.

Jo-Jack put out a hand and Hanna tossed up a duffel containing her clothes. Finding a few well-placed handles and rungs, she pulled herself into the warm cabin. It was a little odd to be facing forward in the front of a car, but this thing was clearly modeled after utility vehicles from the past with two front-facing seats and what looked like a cot in the back. Behind the cab was a closed-in truck bed containing God knows what. Jo-Jack handed her a cappuccino.

"Coffee's a little touch and go once you cross into Nevada. Enjoy it while you can."

Hanna took it happily. "Thanks. So, is this it? Just you and me in a pickup?"

"You were expecting a SEAL Team?"

"I didn't know what to expect."

At that time of day, the streets of San Francisco were crowded with autonomous delivery chassis moving shipping containers. Featureless, wheeled boxes driving with inhuman precision up and down every major artery. Jo-Jack let the truck do its thing and they made their way over the Bay Bridge headed east, constantly inches away from other vehicles as they sped through one of the bridge layers.

He seemed content in silence, which suited Hanna fine at that time of day. As they passed by Oakland, he spoke for the first time.

"Okay, just picking up some supplies."

As they flew north along 80, Hanna saw two windowless RV-shaped vehicles pull into traffic, painted the same black as the truck. They slid in behind the pickup, creating a convoy.

"What's in the support vehicles?" Hanna asked.

"One's liquid hydrogen. It's always best to bring enough fuel for a return trip. This sweet ride is fuel cell only," he said, patting the dash.

"The other?"

"The other is full of stuff we won't need. It's the contingency trailer." He chuckled in a way she was growing fond of.

"I thought you said this was a simple thing now. All it took was paying off the right people."

Jo-Jack looked her in the eyes. "If everything has to go right for a plan to work, you've got yourself a shitty plan."

The drive through Sacramento was uneventful—a couple hours of burned-out roadside from the annual California fires, punctuated by moments of infrastructure. They blew through just in time to miss rush hour.

Gaining elevation, the convoy made its way into the Tahoe State Forest. Hanna ventured into conversation. "Where's home, Jo-Jack?"

"Well, I have a work visa that lets me stay in the Pacific States. So, I keep a trailer up in Bend, Oregon. But my family does still have some land outside of Phoenix. Just not much money to be made that deep into the Southwest these days. So, I keep myself busy doing this kind of work. Taking folks into Idaho, Nevada, sometimes as far as Colorado."

"Much family left?"

"Not much to speak of anymore. Ma and Pa passed away some years back. I have a sister but haven't seen her for a long time." He didn't expand on that, and Hanna didn't push it.

"Wife? Kids?"

Jo-Jack looked at her curiously. "Not that I know of. Your crowd even use those terms anymore?"

Hanna smiled. "We still have kids."

The rise in elevation delivered them into what little forest remained and the change in scenery offered a natural stopping point to the small talk. Late morning rolled in, and they arrived in the town of Truckee.

The town had a perfectly preserved 1950s America look. If it hadn't been for Hanna's trained eye for generative design, she might have thought the businesses were original. They pulled into a diner parking lot and the two follow vehicles drove off, presumably to park somewhere off the main strip.

Over a couple plates of "chicken-fried steak," Hanna picked up where they had left off. "So, what's the family land like back in Arizona?"

"It was a ranch back before I was born. But during my childhood, we converted it into a solar distillation farm. There was a lot of money being thrown around back then trying to make potable water out of city waste. How much you know about the water rights battles?" Hanna shook her head, unable to speak with a mouthful of potatoes and gravy. "Phoenix, Vegas, and LA were all pulling water from the Colorado River. When Lake Mead hit the point of no return, Phoenix got fucked first. LA offered to pump in water from the California desalination network, but things got worse after the split and that level of interstate commerce didn't work out. Long story short, our family pretty much ruined the land with the toxic runoff from making drinking water out of sewage."

"I'm sorry," Hanna said, unsure which part of the global catastrophe she was apologizing for.

"Yeah, it's a sad story, to be sure. As you can imagine, property values only got worse as the waves of Texan refugees rolled in."

They finished, and as Hanna offered to pay for lunch, Jo-Jack laughed and reminded her he was expensing everything to her company. Standing by the pickup, she was struck again by its color—or total lack of color. The vantablack paint soaked up all visible light, reflecting nothing. It was eerie, like someone had just cut the truck shaped hole out of the world with a pair of scissors.

Pulling something from the back, Jo-Jack rounded the truck and tossed her a tac jacket. It looked like a smaller version of what he was wearing.

"Badass. Do I really need this?" Hanna took off her hoodie and threw the jacket on.

"It's a liability thing. Remember what I said about shitty plans?"

"Cool by me. Now I match the truck."

"It has a tactical OS integration I'd like you to install, please."

"Done." Hanna climbed back on board, and they rolled away, the convoy forming up behind them.

They immediately crossed into Nevada and the first thing they saw on the road was a giant truck with an exhaust pipe poking out the top spewing black smoke. Standing in the truck bed were two men with assault rifles slung over their shoulders.

"What in the actual fuck?!" Hanna said.

DOWNTOWN RENO

Reno was an amusement park for Californian debauchery. Locals plied thrill-seeking West Coast do-gooders with drinks before offering all manner of other vices. While gambling, sex work, and drug use were not illegal in the Pacific States, engaging in them openly was not socially acceptable and the wrong act could follow someone for a lifetime. There was also a sense of security offered to tourists by the volume of fake information that spewed out of the Southwestern States. In a practical way, what happened in your search history in Nevada stayed in Nevada.

This ocean of unfiltered, unaccredited information was what necessitated her trip. Moshi Moshi was tasked with branding a variety of Big Water products with the long-dead names of local water sources across Nevada and Arizona. They worked with an affiliated agency based out of Colorado that had been doing the leg work down here to find out what locals generally agreed the names of old rivers, creeks, and lakes had once been. Years ago, when Hanna was just breaking into the industry, she had asked a teammate why the local team didn't just send over the research. Why did someone have to physically go down to watch a presentation about it before the research could be used? They told some story about a Moshi Moshi getting burned in the past and losing a client. It seemed to Hanna that the answer was that it was for show. This was the first time she'd ever been tasked with the trip.

The Denver agency's conference room was above a casino. It seemed impossible to escape the gambling in Reno. Jo-Jack walked her through the gaming floor, a monstrous frenzy of mixed reality. People sat in front of slot machines, giant cartoons erupting as they made incremental winnings. The rush felt as they lost, then won some back, all carefully curated by AI. Everything perfectly calculated to keep people in their seats, even as they lost their shirts. Giant dragons flew through the air above. One machine overflowed with lava as its willing victim hit three bars. A group of dancing elves trailed behind Hanna, coaxing her toward an empty seat.

She blinked off the view from her lenses. The contrast was stark and depressing. People sitting in front of featureless boxes, pulling on handles, chain-smoking nicotine vapes, and slowly giving up everything they had. She looked over at Jo-Jack who was watching her closely.

"Thoughts?" he asked.

"This is fucking grim."

"This isn't the dark side of Reno. You wouldn't believe the kind of shit people with real money come here to do."

"Go on."

"Violence, non-consensual sex, questionable surgery. Whatever you're thinking, it's worse," he said solemnly.

When they arrived at the meeting room, Jo-Jack didn't come in with her, taking a seat at one of the many bars.

The Denver team was a strange flavor of cool— two men and a woman, dressed in perfectly curated hipster-ranch. They wore band t-shirts she didn't recognize and were draped in plaid flannel. Jeans of just the right width hung over dusty Converse shoes. They spoke with the kind of drawl that let them pass unnoticed through the Middle States but wasn't thick enough to get in the way of being taken seriously by someone like Hanna. Hipster-rancher number one took the lead, flipping through slides, calling out the amount of due diligence it took to find historical facts in these parts. It was all very impressive.

"Can I ask you three a question?" Hanna asked after they'd gone over the bulk of the presentation.

"Of course, ma'am," Hipster-rancher one said.

"If there's such a wide interpretation of the truth here, why is it important that we name these things accurately at all? Couldn't we just call them whatever we want and claim it's true, like everyone else seems to be doing with every other historical fact?" The three of them looked at each other.

"In all honesty, ma'am, we just figured it was important to people where you're from. You know, to believe things are true and all," lady hipster-rancher said.

"I suppose it is."

Hanna declined their offer to show her around town, opting instead to find her room and some dinner.

After leaving the meeting, she and Jo-Jack made their way in an Uber to the hotel they would be staying in. After Jo-Jack showed her the way to her room, he retreated to his own. Hanna had also declined his offer to act as tour guide. It was her first time outside of the Pacific States as an adult and she wanted to take it in solo. He'd begrudgingly agreed, so long as she wore her tac jacket. Her room was palatial by the standards of her last hotel. There was a living area with a chair and couch, a separate bedroom, and closets with doors.

She threw the tac jacket on over a formfitting black dress and kept her comfy shoes on. Checking herself out in the mirrored wall by the door she found it to be a fun look, hot even. The walk from her room to the street took her through yet another gaming floor, its mixed reality blaring at her from every angle. The city of Reno opened up in front of her as she stepped outside, its rich tapestry of sin and overeating calling to her. Like, literally calling to her as she walked. Touts stood outside doorways and tried to flick promotions and menus into her field of vision like they were throwing playing cards. The more above-board offers seemed to be at street level. The escort parlors, VR snuff experiences, and pharmacies were up flights of dimly lit stairs.

Hanna found a reputable-looking pharmacy, grabbed a THC vape, a few microdoses of psilocybin, and some amphetamine patches before wandering into a restaurant. Sitting at the counter, she pulled a couple times on the vape and looked over the menu. It was a solid-looking taco joint, the kind you couldn't find in Washington. Looking around she saw everyone eating the same thing. Al pastor slowly roasted on a vertical spit, something her OS quickly told her was a result of Lebanese people immigrating to Mexico centuries ago. She told it to shut up.

The tacos were unlike anything she'd ever tasted. Only after ordering and eating three more did it dawn on her that they were real pork. Hanna didn't identify as vegetarian, but in a practical way she was one. It was a little heartbreaking to walk out realizing she may never taste tacos al pastor like that again. She carried on, knocking back a couple microdoses of psilocybin. They were fast-acting pills, and she felt their subtle effects within minutes.

The edges of the world became a little sharper, the contrast dialed up two degrees. She walked up another dark staircase, paid a cover, and stepped inside a cabaret.

CABARET

anna sat at a small, round table on the main floor, an elevated stage in front of her. Flickering candles lit the room. Her drink arrived right as the headlining act came to the stage. Six women stood silently draped in nothing but sheer white capes. They stood statue-still as old-school laser projectors suddenly shot light at them from the front of the stage. The outlines of the projections matched their silhouettes perfectly so that only their capes lit up in whirling, cosmic patterns. Not a speck of light missed their bodies to hit the wall behind them.

Then music came and they began to dance. They jerked and flowed in a pop-and-lock ballet with stunning precision. Each movement a dancer made was timed with the lightshow. The antique projectors mimicked their dance, only lighting their silhouettes. They glowed. Naked bodies peeked through the translucent capes. It was a kind of old-school mixed reality made far more impressive by the absurd skill of it all. Hanna watched the performance, rapt, the microdose of psychedelics in her system heightening it. The haptics in her little black dress desperately tried to keep up. Waves of eroticism washed over her body.

The show wound to a close and she sat, gathering up the piece of herself. A pianist took the stage and conversation resumed in the dim room. Taking stock of her surroundings for the first time. The upper floor had a balcony and people leaned up against the rail looking down. She people-watched, lazily taking in the crowd, when an unfamiliar OS element entered her vision. It looked like a form of facial recognition, and it called her attention to one of the faces at the balcony. He was a rough-looking man staring right at her. Her tac jacket tightened, and she could feel a rush of adrenaline sobering her up. The same foreign OS element interjected again overlaying into her vision. It showed a map of the club highlighting the three exits. There was a fire escape down a stairwell right behind her. The jacket's haptics were overwhelming and unfamiliar as they became rigid and powerful.

The message was clear. Threat identified. Exit mapped. Hanna stood, trying to look casual, and let her normal OS pay the bill. She walked back toward the bathroom at a normal pace then at the last moment ducked through the fire exit, the tactical OS disabling the alarm for her. Then she ran down a flight of stairs, heart pounding. Her sneaker struck something, an overturned glass on a step, and she was about to fall when her arm flew out to catch the railing. It was as if it had moved on its own, understanding that she was falling before she knew it herself. Back-breaking fall averted, she burst out into the alleyway behind the club. Her pursuer triggered the alarm at the top of the stairs. Without thinking, she pulled an amphetamine patch from her pocket and slapped it on her neck.

She was running. Everything about her movements was new. Hard, precise footfalls and perfect situational awareness flowed through her. She vaulted over a pile of shit and debris, her right hand slamming down into the top of a barrel to throw both her legs over the obstacle. Unbelievably, in the middle of running for her life, her mind told her that she really needed to take this jacket to the gym. Then there were two men standing at the end of the alley. Their bodies framed against her exit, backlit and menacing. She stopped short landing in a braced stance as though she planned on fighting. A laughable idea.

They stepped toward her and her new tactical OS highlighted pipe-like objects in their hands. A suggestion came from somewhere, maybe an auditory stimulus from the OS, she couldn't be sure over the roar of her heartbeat in her ears. "Surrender. Act passive, then break free and run."

Without knowing how, Hanna could sense the man from the club approaching from behind. Driven forward by that thought, she walked toward the two men and the exit of the alleyway. Her hands raised like she was in some 1900s cop show.

As she came close, they raised their metal sticks and she saw an electric spark at the end of each one. Cattle prod, her OS informed her. Then as soon as she came within reach, one of them jabbed her torso with the sparking end of the cattle prod. It made a crack and a little puff of smoke plumed up where it made contact with the tac jacket. The man paused looking confused. He looked down at the end of the cattle prod, then back to Hanna. Realizing the moment had arrived she flung herself into his body. To her surprise her right arm and knee came up. She had a closed fist folded back, almost touching her shoulder. Her knee made contact with his torso and her elbow came down hard on his skull. He folded in on himself like a cardboard cutout. The other one looked on, even more surprised than Hanna by the attack. She took the opportunity to run.

HIGHWAY 580

As Hanna rounded the corner of the alley, a driverless bike pulled up. Then she heard Jo-Jack's voice in her ear, understanding in that moment that it had been his voice in the alley.

"Get the fuck on!"

She jumped on the bike, crouching over the handlebars as it accelerated. It flew through traffic followed by two dark cars. The tac jacket held her down on the bike, keeping her body from catching the wind.

"Show me what's going on," she said either to Jo-Jack or the tactical OS. She wasn't sure at this point.

A video feed came into her vision showing the bike from above. Jo-Jack must have been flying a microdrone above her. The bike, with her terrified body on it, weaved through the late-night traffic of downtown Reno plotting a course between automated party buses and hot tub limos. She was gaining ground, starting to lose the dark cars behind her as they couldn't squeeze between lanes. The drone was only a few meters above her, so she could see clearly when one of the goons leaned out a window of the car, armed with a crossbow.

Hanna screamed as he released a bolt seeing it fly from the drone's vantage point. The sound of her voice woke her from the out-of-body experience of witnessing the scene from above. The projectile narrowly missed her, coming to a stop in the back of a party bus she'd just passed. The electronics on the bus fizzled out as it went dark from the electromagnetic pulse emitted by the bolt.

The bike kept up its breakneck speed and then she was out of range, the cars falling too far behind for a second attempt with the crossbow. Hanna blinked the view from the drone out of her vision and looked at the road ahead. She was staring into the vantablack rear end of one of Jo-Jack's support trailers. A door lowered, something only discernible because the interior of the vehicle was somehow less black than its exterior. The bike popped a wheelie and Hanna screamed for a second time as it leaped into the open door of the automated trailer.

Everything was dark for a moment. Then it wasn't. As the interior lights of the trailer came on, she found herself in a tightly packed storage room. The bike took up most of the floor space.

"I'm going to connect the trailer to the back of the truck. When the hatch opens up, I want you to climb up to the cab," Jo-Jack said in her ear again.

Prying her white knuckles from the handlebars Hanna made her way to the front of the trailer. As she arrived at the featureless front wall, a window opened, exposing the back of the pickup on the other side. She climbed up and into Jo-Jack's truck, gracelessly tumbling into the cot behind the two forward-facing seats.

Jo-Jack was busy working the interface on the truck's dash.

"You, okay?" he asked without looking back.

"Fine," Hanna replied through the pounding of her heart. She sat for a moment, collecting herself in the back, a task hindered by the cocktail of mushrooms, speed, and uncut adrenaline still in her system. After pulling it together, she climbed forward and strapped herself into the passenger seat. The tactical OS showed the vehicle's interface. Jo-Jack was plotting a course out of the city.

"They're following us," he said to her or himself.

"Can you lose them?" she asked.

"I can disable anything chasing us but not in the city. The wrong people could get hurt."

Their convoy sped through traffic headed south and got on the poorly maintained 580. It was a mess of decaying pavement, making the chase harder for the following cars.

"What's the plan?" Hanna asked, after it became clear they wouldn't be losing the pursuers even with the advantage they had on the freeway.

"First thing will be to take out their aerial surveillance."

"Their what?"

"They've got a fixed wing drone in the air. We will need to lose that or there's no way to ditch them. Then we'll continue south for a while and take one of the lesser-used routes back to the Bay Area. It will be a longer trip back, but we should still get there by morning."

"Who the fuck is after me?"

"I'd imagined asking you that question." Jo-Jack looked over at her for the first time since she'd come aboard.

They drove on for some time in silence. Then, upon finding a stretch of relatively smooth road, Jo-Jack kicked the convoy up to a crazy speed. He released a swarm of microdrones from the equipment trailer. As Hanna watched through the display on her tactical OS, the swarm flew in the path of the triangular fixed wing drone flown by their pursuers. The swarm latched onto it and promptly cut it into several pieces. They drove on for a few more miles before taking an exit, feeling secure in the convoy's ability to disappear into the night.

As they turned westward, the two of them exhaled for what felt like the first time ever.

"This is going to be a slower ride back. You might as well try to get some sleep," Jo-Jack said, gesturing to the cot in the back.

"I'm vibrating over here."

"Well, it's going to be a dark and boring drive compared to the last hour. Neither one of us is going to have much to do. We've definitely lost them."

"I've got an idea," Hanna said, leaning over to grab him by the front of the shirt. She pulled his body into her, surprising him with her mouth on his. The sudden and severe arousal was clearly triggered by her brush with death. After getting over his surprise Jo-Jack leaned in eagerly. They fumbled with each other's clothes, falling back into the cot behind them.

There was a hunger to it, a frantic pace. Hanna slid down, suddenly desperate to taste him. They contorted every which way on the narrow bed, finding new positions over and over again. She could feel herself using the experience to flush everything she'd been through out of her system. The freakish hyper-awareness she'd felt in the alley showing up again as they fucked.

Then a deep dreamless sleep.

NORTH BEACH

Jo-Jack and Hanna sat across from each other drinking coffee near the vactrain station in North Beach. Hanna felt remarkably well rested.

Jo-Jack hadn't slept after their fun in the cab of the truck and looked rough. Handsome but tired. "So, someone serious is after you, huh?" he said over the rim of a cappuccino.

"It's beginning to look that way."

"Feel like filling me in? I'm going to need to offer some kind of explanation to your employer. That drone swarm will be noticeable on my invoice."

"This may turn out to be a the-less-you-know-the-better kind of a thing. How much do you value plausible deniability?" Hanna asked seriously.

"I'm more about knowing if that's on the table," he replied.

Hanna paused thinking about the implications of telling Jo-Jack everything. She'd only known this guy for a day. On the other hand, during that twenty four hour period they'd slept together, he'd offered to lie for her, and it was very likely that he'd saved her life. She decided to tell him the truth.

"Well... I have a couple of friends in Seattle. I'm pretty sure they've stolen the most valuable piece of intellectual property on Earth and the word is out. My first thought was that the company they stole it from is after them and coming at me because I'm an easy target on this trip. But if that was the case, I don't think we would have escaped last night. So that only leaves one option. Some other person— or more likely a group of people have figured out what my friends have and want it for themselves." Hanna was putting this together for the first time as she said it out loud.

"This thing they stole—it's worth killing for?"

"It's the Alphabet master behaviour algo," Hanna said.

Jo-Jack stared at her, mouth hanging open. They sat in silence for a full minute.

"What are they going to do with it? I mean, how did they even..."

"Believe it or not, they're using it to make art." She couldn't help but laugh.

"What in the ever-living fuck?" Jo-Jack stopped short again.

"Right? As of a week ago, this is somehow my life. Honestly, if they were doing anything else with it, I think Alphabet would have found out by now and brought in PSAF to throw them down a deep hole." Hanna said, using the colloquial term for the Pacific States Autonomous Forces.

"And just how are you involved?"

"I helped them design a logo. That's it. But that was enough for me to figure out what they've done. What I can't figure out is how anyone knows about it. Unless... on the train ride down here. I was reading all the hype they'd generated and had my OS search for any info on the algo theft. They must have been sitting close enough on the train ride

to hack my OS. Then they blackmailed Mason..."
Hanna was speaking to herself as it fell into place.

"Wait, who's *they* in this scenario?"

"Big Water," Hanna said.

=

She had kissed the flabbergasted Jo-Jack goodbye, taking him up on his offer to write off the attempted kidnapping as a routine assault and car chase. They made vague plans to keep in touch, but she wouldn't have blamed him for never wanting to hear from her again. Either way, she felt certain that their secret was safe with him.

On the train, Hanna wondered what the hell was next. The vactrain didn't offer much of a view, being inside a giant pneumatic tube and all. It left her with a feeling of stasis, like what being on hold must have felt like back when that was a thing. There was no way she was going to dig into OTAKU in a crowded space like this so that left work.

Hopping into her company account, she was slammed with a pile of messages from HR. It seemed that Jo-Jack was not a procrastinator where paperwork was concerned. He must have uploaded a report from the cafe. Moshi Moshi was already pushing her into a mental health funnel, explaining that she wouldn't have access to any of her work projects until she'd been cleared—some kind of automated liability process mandated by their insurance. Hanna held the bridge of her nose between her thumb and forefinger, exhaling audibly.

She remembered the archived message from Mason. Desperate for anything that might inform her plans upon returning home she had her OS recover it. She had brushed it aside back in her hotel two nights ago without realizing he'd sent it from his personal account.

Mason sat in a vacant industrial space on a metal chair. His face was bloodied, and he looked unconscious. Text appeared on the screen, cycling in one sentence at a time. The first thing Hanna noticed was the styling of it—a large, white font, all caps and sized with a nice eye for kerning and scale. It had the look of a well laid-out magazine ad. She shook off the realization that the video was made with a design algo and came back to reading the text.

"We can't find your friends yet. But this co-worker has given us enough to start looking. Have them deliver us a copy of the stolen algo and it will be like none of this ever happened." The video stopped.

Hanna spent the last hour of the ride back to Seattle thinking that she must have set this in motion by ignoring this message in San Francisco and allowing herself to get hacked on the vactrain.

FIRST HILL WALK

Stepping off the train was like waking up from a dream. Hanna walked up the steps of the Union Station and got shit-scared. Her experience from the night before collided with the image of Mason's bloody face in her mind and she just froze, unable to think of what to do next. She was under clear instructions not to return to the office until her psychiatric evaluation was complete, and Xin-Lao's status had them as unavailable. In the end, she just went on autopilot and got a car home.

It felt like Hanna had been gone for months as she walked in the front door of her building. Her OS grabbing a bunch of notifications, sorting them according to relevance and due dates. As she went through her usual routine of skimming her missed mail in the elevator, she looked up at her reflection in the mirrored doors. She was still wearing the black tac jacket Jo-Jack had lent her for the Reno run. She hadn't noticed she was wearing it during the ride up on the vactrain. Jo-Jack must have been looking at her the whole time they'd had coffee, wondering if she was going to give it back. Actually, he seemed like the kind of person who would have said something. Maybe he intended for her to keep it? Maybe he just added it to Moshi Moshi's invoice?

She walked into her place, throwing her bag down on the floor by the entryway and went to the kitchen. Her grocery list had been fulfilled in time for her return. Hanna pulled a pack of miso pearls from the crate and popped two into hot water. They dissolved, transforming into a mug of soup. Walking over to her couch, she caught a glimpse of the tidy bot dragging her duffel down the hall into the bedroom. The reacher arm that looked like its head and long neck dragged the bag across the floor like a body.

It was raining. The turn of seasons that came to the Pacific Northwest near the end of September was finally upon the city. Seattle's climate shift had been one of the more subtle across the States, but it was still noticeable. Summer ended with a few weeks of smoke as wildfires crept further north each year. Then perfect weather for a few weeks, then the rain. That weather that characterized Seattle—the reason so many used to hate it—was now something people risked everything for. Migrating across state lines, dodging border security drones, losing the opportunity to work legally. The Pacific States had an open border policy for climate refugees on paper, but it wasn't that cut and dry in practice.

She was in no state to start the process of getting back to work so Hanna put off the insurance-appointed AI's offer to start her counseling session and did the only thing she could think of. She set out to find her friends.

The walk from her building in Eastlake to the Sorcery Outlet was about an hour on foot. Hanna felt like she was on the edge of throwing up, so she forced herself to walk. It took her through Capitol Hill and then along the edge of First Hill, an area once dominated by medical complexes and hospitals. The space needed for that industry had shrunk significantly over the last few decades. Realtime biometric data paired with a personal OS had changed things. The sprawling infrastructure used to simply diagnose a human body was no longer needed. Around that same time, the world developed a commitment to reusing old construction as the price of concrete skyrocketed. So, the monolithic, Gotham-themed buildings were still there housing datacenters with stories and stories of Amazon server racks. It gave the neighborhood an even more desolate feel than when it had catered to the sick and infirm. You could walk for blocks without finding something to eat now.

Hanna arrived at Xin-Lao's loft. Earl was surprised when she knocked on their door unannounced. "Well, aren't you a sight for sore eyes," he said, sweeping her up in a big hug.

"It's really good to find you here." She was worried that the three of them may have disappeared without a trace.

"Come inside. I will feed you." Earl grinned.

Sitting at the kitchen counter, Hanna's stomach relaxed a little for the first time that day.

Earl tossed food in a wok and looked over his shoulder at her. "So, everything's turned to shit, huh?" He smiled as he spoke.

"Seems that way," Hanna replied. Then, after a moment's consideration. "Do you know if it's safe for us to talk in here?"

"Yevgeny is privacy obsessed. From what I understand, this place has security protocols with layers of redundancy that would make the average person call him paranoid. They made me say that. I called him paranoid. Seems like he might have the last laugh now though."

"Do you know about what they've done?" Hanna said, now speaking between mouthfuls of fried rice.

"No. And please don't tell me. Not knowing was really helpful when those goons came to our door yesterday. They must have had some military-grade software in their eyes. They could see I was telling the truth when I told them I didn't know where my lovers had run to." Earl had a disarming way about him. He felt like a childhood friend.

"So, you don't know where I can find them?" She couldn't mask her disappointment.

"I surely do not. However, Xin-Lao did leave you something." He turned his massive frame, disappearing into one of the back bedrooms.

He returned with a large sheet of paper. It was Hanna's printout of the OTAKU logo. Slapping it down on the counter, he motioned for her to turn it over and walked away. On the back, written in lipstick, was a set of GPS coordinates: 47°36'00.7"N 122°20'01.0"W.

CAPITOL HILL ALLEYWAY

Hanna spent the next couple of days unable to sleep from anxiety and dragging her heels on the psychiatric evaluation for work. She paced around her neighborhood while fretting about what to do and scanning the culture lists to see what the city was saying about OTAKU. She kept the piece of paper with the GPS coordinates folded up behind some frozen fruit in her freezer, marveling at the security of storing information in an analog way.

On the morning of the third day, she was able to confirm that she was being followed. The person tailing her was good, using reflective surfaces to keep Hanna in their field of vision without ever revealing themself fully. Without the advantage of the tactical OS, her feeling of being followed would never have been confirmed.

Walking into her usual cafe on Capitol Hill, Hanna ordered two cups of coffee and mapped out a plan. She headed west down Pine, moving at a brisk pace, then took a sudden right into an alley where she ducked into a doorway. Enough time passed for her to second-guess herself. Then Tapeesa rounded the corner, walking right by the little doorway Hanna was standing in. She was moving quickly, concerned that she'd lost her target. Hanna mustered up all of her courage and offered her one of the to go cups.

"Coffee?"

Tapeesa turned, surprised but hiding it well.

"Thank you," she said slowly.

"I don't know where they are. You can stop following me. Although I will say this is a step up from being abducted." Hanna was proud of how calm she sounded.

"Yes. That was only an option outside of the Pacific States. It would create a lot of noise here."

Tapeesa spoke casually—unapologetic but not threatening.

The woman stepped into the wide doorway with Hanna, leaning against the other side of the arch as she took a sip of coffee.

"Then how did you get away with kidnapping Mason?" Hanna asked.

"You haven't been back to work yet." It was a statement. "He's there, unharmed."

"The video wasn't real? How's that possible? My OS would have caught a deep fake."

"I didn't say it was fake. It's remarkably easy to trick an operating system. Sometimes you just need to go analog." She smiled for the first time, pleased with herself.

"Fuck me. You used makeup for the bruises? But how did you get him into the chair for it?"

Hanna was caught up in the brilliance for a moment, almost forgetting that this woman was responsible for hacking her OS and hiring Middle State goons to do God knows what to her. It was just too clever not to admire. They'd faked the video the old-fashioned way, knowing that an algo watching it would only spot digital alterations.

"We paid him," Tapeesa said matter-of-factly.

"But you attempted my abduction."

"Your trip into Nevada presented a unique opportunity."

"An opportunity you orchestrated by requesting that I go there in the first place," Hanna spat, finding her outrage.

"Of course we did. Do you understand what a singular moment this is? Your friends pulled off the biggest heist in modern history and they've done it largely undetected. That algo could do so much in the right hands. They're using it to create art. Fucking art!"

"And Big Water is the right hands in this example?"

"Our people have been the victims of humanity's largest genocide, followed by hundreds of years of cultural and economic oppression. It's only in our lifetimes, yours and mine, that some of us have begun to climb out of that. We *are* the right hands."

Hanna paused for a moment.

"You said they pulled this off undetected. I've figured it out. It sure seems like Mason has. And of course you and your people have as well. That's hardly nobody."

"So far, it's undetected by the people they stole it from, and we've bought Mason's silence. But it's going to come out if they expose more people to it. It was clear what they'd done when I went to the last exhibit. If they do another show like that, it's over, and this treasure isn't worth anything if they get hunted down and locked up." She finished her coffee and tossed it into a nearby compost dumpster.

"I don't know what you expect me to do about all this. I just designed the logo. I'm barely involved," Hanna said.

"Stop them from whatever they're planning next. For the love of all that's holy, convince them to sell it to us. They can take the unreasonable amount of money we'll happily pay and go live their lives. This is the only way they get out of this situation with their freedom. You and I both know that the moment Alphabet sees what they've done, they will call in PSAF to clean up the whole mess," Tapeesa said. She was referring to the Pacific States Autonomous

Forces, the drone army built to monitor the borders of Washington, Oregon, and California.

Tapeesa walked off, leaving her in the alleyway where she'd executed her ambush. Hanna stood there in wonder at the speed at which someone could lose the upper hand in a situation. The element of surprise was really nothing in the face of actual surprising information.

MOSHI MOSHI PHONE ROOM

By the following day Hanna was sure she no longer had a tail. However, she couldn't put off the AI pestering her to take her psychiatric evaluation any longer. She sat in her living room and let it happen.

"Hey there, Hanna," the AI said, speaking through her home audio system. Its voice was accompanied by a friendly mixed reality cloud. The cloud hovered in her living room, designed to give her something to talk to. "So, I hear you had a real scare on your trip to Reno."

"There was a thing that happened for sure," Hanna said to the cloud therapist.

"Did you fear for your life at any point?" it asked.

"No. No, I don't think that I did." She needed to consider this. "It all happened so fast, I guess I didn't have time for that."

"Did you feel helpless? Like you had no control over what was happening to you?"

"I most certainly did not." Hanna almost laughed at the idea. She'd never felt so powerful in her life.

"Have you been reliving the experience in any way? Playing it over in your mind?" The cloud's voice was designed to be supportive, non-threatening.

"Nope. I keep forgetting that it happened, actually."

"What about dreams? Are you having any trouble sleeping?"

"I'm sleeping like a baby."

The questions went on for a while in this vein. Hanna answered them honestly, assuming her algo interviewer would be able to tell if she didn't.

"So, it seems like you're doing pretty well, all things considered. Do you mind if I ask you one more question, Hanna?"

"Ask away."

"Have you left the house without that military combat jacket since your trip?"

The question brought her up short. "Ummm, I haven't. I hadn't given it much thought if I'm being honest."

"That jacket is a weapon. Wearing it around town might make people uncomfortable. Have you noticed if that's been happening?"

"I don't think so. I mean, I haven't noticed anyway." As she was saying this she thought back to Jo-Jack walking into the bar on the night they met, turning heads as he strolled across the rooftop in what she thought of as a conspicuous get-up at the time.

"I'm going to clear you to go back to work, but I want you to give some thought as to why you're still wearing the jacket, Hanna."

"I guess I will. Thanks."

"Do I have your permission to share my assessment with your employer?"

"You do."

"Great, thanks for taking the time for this today. You can go back in to work as early as tomorrow morning. Feel free to call on me if you need anything."

"I'll keep that in mind." Hanna said.

Then the therapy cloud vanished, and Hanna was alone in her living room again.

=

She woke up the next morning thinking back to the conversation with the therapy cloud. Something about the whole encounter in Reno had left her feeling empowered. When it had asked if she had felt helpless, the memory of her escape in the alleyway came back in full. She has been a badass. Now, with the fear of abduction alleviated during her talk with Tapeesa, Hanna felt different. Something had shifted inside, making her powerful. She turned it up in her haptics.

Returning to work, Hanna made a point of carrying the jacket in a bag rather than wearing it into the office. Co-workers welcomed her back as she sat at the team desks. It seemed like people didn't know she had been placed on a mental health leave. She struggled to find motivation for work. Projects had piled up in her absence, but she couldn't shake the feeling that reviewing some generative design output just wasn't worth her time. It was hard to muster up any fucks about some soulless design—something that didn't inspire OTAKU. She stood and turned to walk out of the office, throwing on the tac jacket as she did.

Stepping away from the desk Hanna felt a hand on her shoulder. "How'd you like my performance, sweetheart?" Mason said into her ear.

Without thinking she stood, spun toward him, and stepped into his face.

He was taken aback but managed to maintain a disgusting smile.

"Come with me," Hanna said and strode off to a nearby meeting room.

The two of them stood close together in the soundproofed call booth, its only window facing an exterior wall of the building. Hanna glared at Mason. He smirked back.

"What the fuck do you want from me? You've already sold out my friends and drove them into hiding," she said.

"Here's the way I see it, love. One word from me and all of you are truly fucked. I don't know how you and your friends did it. Stealing that algo was really impressive but you're in a mountain of shit. So, you're going to do what I've been wanting for months now."

"And that is?"

"Come on. I want your tight ass. It's pretty fucking clear. I'll tell you what, you get on your knees right now and blow me and I won't report your friends to the police."

Hanna looked into his eyes. There was nothing there. On an intellectual level, she understood that horrible people were themselves driven by suffering, that they acted out in a desperate attempt to hide from their own pain. But she couldn't see any of that in Mason's eyes. There was only vacancy.

She punched him hard in the stomach. While wearing the jacket, movement came naturally, feeling powerful and practiced. He doubled over, winded. Hanna grabbed his head by the hair and shoved him down to the ground. Then she bent down to his level.

"You think I don't know about the money you took from Big Water? I know you can't go to the police. You're in their pocket now. They'd end you. You are never going to speak to me again. Do you understand?"

"Yes." He looked up at her, confused and scared. Unable to catch his breath.

Hanna stayed there for a moment, crouched over him as he lay in the fetal position. He kept looking at her, expecting her to say something else. Realizing that things were only getting weirder, she stood up and left.

She walked down the covered walkway leading away from the Moshi Moshi office.

"Hey, therapy cloud, you there?"

"I am. What's up?" The disembodied voice came through the bone induction audio in her jacket.

"You were wrong. I'm not ready to go back to work."

PIKE PLACE MARKET

She strode away from her office. There was something so intoxicating about being angry and right at the same time. With a bunch of adrenaline in her system and no plans, Hanna did the only thing she could think of and went to the gym.

She stood on the starting platform of the obstacle course, jacket on, body twitching with anticipation for the signal to run. The oldschool green bulb lit up and Hanna threw herself at the course. Every jump felt shorter than she remembered. She flew through the air, grabbing handholds with one hand and propelling herself over obstacles that she had to haul her body over in the past. She felt both powerful and light on her feet driving through, over, and under everything in the course without thought or hesitation.

Then she stood at the warped wall, the final challenge and one that she had never conquered in the years she'd been coming to this gym. She threw herself at it, sprinting into the sloped curve at the bottom and making it at least two steps higher up the vertical face before leaping to catch the lip at its top. Both hands landed squarely on the ledge, and she pulled her body up and over the ledge before walking to the timer button on the raised platform and slapping it triumphantly.

She walked out of the gym without even breaking a sweat, wondering if she would ever take the jacket off again.

=

It was late morning and Hanna hadn't eaten. She headed north up to Pine Street and turned toward the water. The old sign for Pike Place Market grew out of the distance. The market had been spared from rising sea levels due to a hill along the city's coastline. Where it once looked down on a waterfront commercial district, there were now lapping waves.

The charm of the place came from its largely unchanged feel. The market had survived malignant capitalism, gentrification, and climate change—

all while sticking with a business model as old as agriculture. Part tourist trap, part functioning local shopping plaza, Pike Place seemed immune to the rising tide of generative branding. The long rows of flower booths and fruit stalls didn't even have names.

Vendors stood by piles of pears, offering freshly cut slices to passersby. Bakers, baristas, jewelers, and buskers all plied their trade along the crowded passageway. Hanna found a pastry and made her way to one of the patios that had been added to the roof of the market. Looking south along the water's edge, she could see how drastically the ocean had changed downtown. City streets only sat a foot below the water, but below that was the world of submerged basements and underground sidewalks turned tunnels. The buildings below the tideline had been stripped of anything worth salvaging decades ago and now loomed there, useless.

Hanna looked around to confirm she was alone and pulled out the GPS coordinates from Xin-Lao. Her OS read them and placed a pin over the location off in the distance. It was definitely in one of those submerged buildings. At first, she thought it might be the tunnel where Yevgeny had held the exhibit, but it was too far from shore.

Hanna's first thought was to call an AirLyft to get dropped off on the roof. But when she tried, she found that it wouldn't take her into the abandoned area offshore, which made sense when she thought about it. Predicting her next search, her OS pulled up a list of boat tours operating in the area. A small but consistent tourist trade had sprung up catering to people who wanted to sail among the flooded buildings of Pioneer Square. Hanna chartered a whole boat, so she'd have the ride to herself and set off for the dock listed in the confirmation message.

The dock was located on the lowest floor of the market itself. The captain of her little vessel was just a boy, a teenager who introduced himself as Jamail. Hanna stood on the dock as he gestured for her to come aboard looking grateful for a chartered gig on a slow day.

"Jamail, I have a proposition for you," Hanna said.

"Oh?" The young man looked cautiously optimistic.

"I'd like to pay you double, but I'll need you to enter that I was a no-show in your logs."

"Seems like the kind of shit that could get me in trouble with my boss," he replied.

"Triple."

"Done."

Hanna received a notice that her reservation was canceled and transferred the payment to Jamail's personal account. The eight-foot-long catamaran had almost no hull below the waterline. It was the kind of craft she imagined well-to-do people raced around lakes. She sat on the bench near its bow and Jamail cast off from the dock.

A silent electric motor propelled them through the shallow water. She could see the streets a foot or so below the surface and it felt peaceful in a way Hanna hadn't expected. Once Jamail cut the engine and hoisted the sails, they started moving quickly and Hanna found herself taken with the experience. Jamail told her stories of the area's history. She half-listened to tales of gold rush prospectors, bootleggers, and brothels as the empty buildings slid by in the eerie seascape.

As they approached the building her OS had pinned, Hanna saw an old metal fire escape running up its side. The lowest landing was within reach from the water level.

"Okay, Jamail. This is where we part ways," Hanna said, gesturing to the fire escape.

"What the fuck? Are you crazy? I can't wait around for you out here and no one will come back to pick you up."

"Then I guess it's a good thing we never met."

Jamail reluctantly gave her a boost and Hanna pulled herself up. Standing on the rusting metal of the fire escape, she watched the young man push off. He had probably thought she was eccentric before, but now there was only fear on his face. As she pulled away, he looked like a sailor dropping someone off on a remote iceberg, like she had just made him complicit in her death. The waves lapped below the thin grate at her feet. Hanna climbed up and started to second-guess herself.

PIONEER SQUARE OFFICE

The roof of the building was in surprisingly good shape compared to the fire escape she'd just climbed. As Hanna walked around, she noticed air ducts and a small structure with a door had been added recently. She walked over to it and pulled on the handle, finding it unlocked. It housed a spiral staircase.

The long staircase wound down the inside of a massive, corrugated tube taking Hanna down to what she assumed was the basement. She walked through the door at the bottom into a fully furnished, modern office.

Full spectrum lights made it feel like daylight was flooding in through the windows, but outside revealed an underwater landscape complete with schools of fish and wandering crabs. There were desks, working walls, conference rooms, everything except people. The place was large. Hanna stood there, unable to believe it, until she remembered Yevgeny's passing comment about some friends of his who were testing an underwater real estate idea. This must have been their venture-backed prototype.

Xin-Lao appeared from one of the conference rooms, arms outstretched. "My lovely! You made it!" Their oversized tent coat shimmered, evoking the seascape outside.

The two of them hugged, then kissed for a bit.

"We need to talk. A lot has happened," Hanna said.

"Absolutely." Xin-Lao was pulling her toward the room they'd emerged from, getting more excited along the way. "Yevgeny has been making interesting discoveries. He's been learning more about the capabilities of the Alphabet algo with each exhibit. Now he's figured out how to use it to create curated emotional experiences using people's haptics."

"Please tell me you two aren't down here planning another OTAKU."

"It is already in motion," Yevgeny said as they walked into the boardroom which, judging from the smell, he'd been living in. Along with its standard conference furniture the room contained an air mattress, a duffle bag of clothes, shopping bags full of food, and an old-school projector. On the wall opposite the door, Yevgeny was working on actual lines of code, something Hanna had never seen. He typed on a laser projected keyboard, the red light coming from a little cube that drew the keys of an antiquated typewriter on the conference table. The spectacle looked like something from a period drama. He spoke to her without breaking a keystroke.

"The implications of this are staggering. The algo was designed to pull emotional experiences off people. We all knew that. How many times have we all been served up an ad on the street to help with a bad day? But what I didn't know, couldn't have known, was that this thing works just as well when you flip the input and output."

"What are you trying to tell me, Yevgeny?"

"The algo is just as effective at suggesting emotional experiences to someone as it is at understanding them."

Xin-Lao smiled at Hanna, giving her time to take the idea in.

"Okay, I clearly don't know as much about the technical details as the two of you, but I've always been under the impression that there's no way to look at an AI algo and understand what it can or can't do. I mean they're a black box, right? That's what we all learned in school. And the Alphabet algo is famous for this. It's used by every major company around the world to pull data off people and no one knows how it works. How could you have figured this out?"

"We just tried it," Xin-Lao said.

"We didn't need to look inside it at all. I wrote an application to run emotional data in the opposite direction, ported the algo in—gave it access to some clothes and flipped the switch, so to speak." With this last statement Yevgeny finally turned to look at Hanna.

"Fuck me," Hanna said. "So, you're saying that all you have to do is flip the flow of information and this same algo, the one that the whole world pretty much runs on, can make someone feel a particular way?" Then, after a moment's pause, she blurted, "Wait, what do you mean you tried it? Who did you try it on?"

"I went first," Xin-Lao said cheerfully.

"What did it feel like?" Hanna asked cautiously.

"Subtle but real. We tried all kinds of things. It can make you feel joyous, sad, inspired, even kind of spiritual with the right mix of emotions," they said.

Hanna sat heavily in one of the chairs around the conference table, her fingers finding her temples as her head fell into her hands.

"You understand that one more exhibit will mean exposure? I have so much to tell you about the people who are already after us, but they'll be nothing compared to the PSAF that Alphabet will send once it's clear what you've done," Hanna said.

"What if this is what the Alphabet algo is actually used for? What if we're all being manipulated like this all the time? We have to call attention to this. It has to come out now that we understand what it is," Xin-Lao said.

"So what? You're a couple of whistleblowers now?"

"Back during the rise of Web 2, people had their first real interactions with AI. It was the very beginning of the generations-long exchange of value we're still participating in. The deal our grandparents made, to trade their personal data for services, was the precursor to the advertising we are stuck with now. But if this is real, we're not just being mined for data so they can sell us stuff. Our emotional states are being tweaked as well. For all we know, most of the world hasn't had a feeling that was purely their own for decades. I'm not going to sit on that information," Yevgeny said.

"I mean, we use our own haptics to modulate emotional experiences all the time," Hanna said, half to herself.

"And the reason we're all cool with that is we can still fool ourselves into believing those modulated emotional experiences are still our own."

"Are you saying this is happening? Or that it might be happening?" Hanna asked.

"Yevgeny figured this out in a couple of days. You really think that the powers behind it don't know?

The whole thing is simple enough to run in the background of our lives, just making all the ads that we get served even more effective. None of the advertisers or agencies would need to be in on it," Xin-Lao said.

"If you two plan on putting on another exhibit, there's going to be nowhere to hide. The whole city is waiting for the next one. Alphabet is going to find out."

The three of them spent the day talking and watching Yevgeny work. Hanna filled the two of them in on all that had happened during her trip to Reno and her encounter with Tapeesa from Big Water on the streets of Capitol Hill.

Over the course of the day, it became clear that Xin-Lao and Yevgeny were willing to sacrifice everything if it meant getting their opus into the world. It also became clear that Hanna was not. "Okay, if you're set on this you need to have an exit planned. I may be able to help with that," Hanna said.

〓

The dim ocean light played over Xin-Lao's hip, along their flat stomach and chest, creating a silhouette like a brush mark, painting the body's contours in a single stroke. Hanna traced it with a finger, starting at the nipple, then meandering down between their legs. She fell deep into her lover's body again and again. The two of them moved in and around each other wordlessly. The sounds of their sex carried through the office. Then they both slept.

Waking in the early morning light, Hanna rolled off the air mattress trying not to wake Xin-Lao. She threw on a pair of panties and wrapped herself in an oversized sweater she found in a duffel bag. Walking out into the office, she discovered the morning light was actually artificial and cast by the full spectrum LEDs embedded in the office's window frames. The view outside was still dark.

Following the faint sounds from the kitchen area, she found Yevgeny making coffee. He looked at her fondly, something he had never done before, and handed her a cup. He leaned in and kissed her on the cheek.

"You're a part of the family now," he said, and they sat in a couple of chairs by a window.

"Did you sleep well?" Hanna asked.

"The nap pods in this place could be better."

"Thanks for giving us the bed."

"It was my pleasure." He smiled and then said, "So what's your plan to get us into Canada?"

"I met a couple of interesting people on my trip down to Reno. I reached out last night to call in favors. I don't know a lot about disappearing, but these guys have some ideas and I trust them."

"We're putting our lives in your hands. How confident are you?" Yevgeny said matter-of-factly.

"Well, Jo-Jack I'd trust with my life. By that I mean, I'd trust him with it again. The other guy, Burtrum, I don't know as well. But if we're looking for someone to help you two unplug, he's the least plugged-in person I've ever met. If you have anyone you'd trust more with this, by all means bring 'em in."

"I don't have friends like this."

"I think the bigger question here is this. Are you willing to trade the most valuable thing you've ever had in your possession for protection once you're north of the border?"

"If it means we get to do this last exhibit, yes. I'm ready to give it away."

INTERNATIONAL DISTRICT STATION

The three of them left the submerged office by way of a tunnel emerging just above the high-tide line into the International District. Hanna wore the jacket. Chinatown swallowed them as they walked inland. Signage threw itself at Hanna as it had her whole life, but it felt different now. It reminded her of the gaming floors in Reno. Aggressive dumplings, dancing medicinal roots, and off-brand electronics stirred up feelings in her chest and invaded her vision. She turned it all down, overly sensitive to the idea that her feelings might be influenced with each passing mixed reality ad.

Hanna had always felt cool for liking this part of town, like she was in the know. She fancied herself someone who found pockets of treasure in the less trodden streets of her city. As the three of them strode purposefully toward a lesser known and therefore superior ramen shop, she questioned everything. Was this feeling of exclusivity that accounted for so much of her identity seeded by an algo?

Yevgeny, Xin-Lao, and Hanna ran through the plan one more time between slurps of noodles. Then, bowls drained, Yevgeny kicked off the final exhibit.

He removed a silver pouch from his jacket pocket and unfolded the top. Reaching into it with two fingers, he pulled out an ancient cellular phone. Hanna had only ever seen them in VR serials. It was larger than she expected, like it would be hard to use with one hand. The screen covering one side of the phone lit up as Yevgeny placed it on the table between them. He drew a pattern on the screen with his finger and it unlocked. On the phone's display, there was one lonely icon. Yevgeny tapped it and the same software he'd been working on in the underwater office sprung into life. Colored lines of code scrolled upwards on a black background.

"You need to plug that old brick into something?" Hanna asked.

"No. I've rigged it to work with our current satellite connections. The only thing keeping it from connecting was this Faraday bag," he said, shaking the silver pouch. "There's no getting the toothpaste back in the tube now though. These old phones are very easy to locate and track."

"Well, then, let's get this show on the road." Xin-Lao stood.

The three of them walked out the restaurant door. Hanna went back into Chinatown and her two companions walked off to find a blimp.

=

The letters loomed over the International District rail station: OTAKU. They floated, visible to anyone who had been following the hype. So pretty much everyone. Hanna looked up at them nervously.

Tapeesa strolled up. "It's nice to see you again, Hanna."

"Thanks for coming."

"So, you and your friends are really doing this?" she asked.

"To be clear, they're doing this. I'm the idiot who designed the logo. You are going to help Yevgeny and Xin-Lao not get deported from Canada once we smuggle them across the border. Just so we all remember our roles."

"They agreed to give us the algo?"

"Yevgeny has agreed to hand over a copy in exchange for their protection. But I have a favor to ask as well."

"Oh?"

"I'm planning on staying in Seattle and so is their housemate, Earl."

"We're aware of Earl."

"I'm complicit in this crime and he has nothing to do with it. What can you do for the two of us so that we don't have to look over our shoulders for the rest of our lives?"

"I already have a team tearing down your search history and rebuilding it clean to shield you. We can get started on Earl. Is there anything else?" Tapeesa asked.

"I don't know. How about a promotion?" Hanna joked, trying to make light of the ease with which Tapeesa seemed to grant wishes.

"That shouldn't be a problem," she replied. Dead serious. "How do you plan to get them across the border?"

"Believe it or not, I have a couple of guys that are uniquely qualified for that. They're on their way as we speak. Are you going to stick around for the exhibit?"

"I'm afraid not. We have a lot to prepare, and this is going to happen fast now. I'm sure this goes without saying, but our organization will have nothing to do with them until they cross the border. Getting on the wrong side of PSAF would cripple our business."

"I assumed as much," Hanna said.

"Let's just pray they don't get caught," Tapeesa replied before shaking her a head and turning to walk away.

=

Hanna looked up at the logo she designed. The thing she'd done for a crush that had somehow led to all this in a matter of days. Yevgeny's notification popped up. *You came to see this. Agree to installation?* Which she did.

A crowd was trickling into the courtyard above the light rail station. One by one Hanna felt their arrival. A tiny chord struck in her with the addition of each person to the growing group. She felt a hidden layer of meaning revealing itself like an orchestra, one instrument joining in after another to perform a symphony. Hanna found herself struck with significance. A giant murder of crows migrated overhead from one part of the city to another, their movements betraying an underlying intelligence. Light fell through the clouds in perfect Euclidean angles. The feeling of subtle separation Hanna had felt her whole life melted away. The crowd began to walk.

Intellectually, she knew her experience was manufactured. She, just like everyone else, had agreed to download Yevgeny's application. And she, more than anyone else, understood that he was using the Alphabet algo to seed a spiritual awakening. But none of that understanding was saving her from the experience. A powerful feeling of connection and community engulfed the group of people becoming more pronounced with each additional member. The experience reminded her of trances described by ancient Sufi mystics. Without warning she remembered a poem by Hafiz that her dad used to read out loud when she was a kid.

God and I have become

like two giant fat people

living in a tiny boat.

We keep bumping

into each other

and laughing.

The exhibit moved toward downtown led by people walking organically up one of the city's major arteries. The OTAKU logo floating along with them like they were pulling a giant balloon. It had grown into an unstructured parade, a city-wide love-filled protest. Looking back, Hanna could no longer see the end. They had taken over the street. Autonomous cars, delivery cubes, and other vehicles were at a standstill. Just a river of people flowing into the heart of the city. Everywhere she turned people were laughing, weeping, walking arm in arm, exalted.

Looking forward through the crowd, Hanna saw Earl's giant torso from behind. She ran up to him and jumped, throwing her arms around his body. Without breaking stride, he grabbed her legs, pulling her up into a piggyback without even knowing it was her. Hanna kissed him on the cheek, and he turned to see her face.

"I am so intensely happy to see you," Earl said.

"I know, right? Aren't I delightful?"

"You truly are." He swung her body around his giant frame, hooking one arm behind her back and the other under her knees until he was carrying her like a bride over the threshold of their new home.

Hanna put her arms around his neck and nuzzled him. "You know what all this means, right?" she whispered.

"They're leaving." He wore a sad smile.

"It was the only way. They needed to do this last exhibit and there's no way it goes unnoticed. Both of them will have to leave the country tonight."

"Do you know where they are now?"

Hanna looked up and Earl followed her gaze. Gliding above the crowd was a sightseeing airship, the kind tourists hopped on and off to see the city's landmarks in a day.

"Did you know you can just rent one of those all to yourself?" she chuckled.

SPACE NEEDLE

It took an hour for the parade to find its way to Seattle Center. Hanna arrived hand in hand with Earl into a heaving mass of people gathered around the Space Needle. They moved through the sea of bodies toward its edge hoping to meet Xin-Lao and Yevgeny as they touched down so they could leave together to meet Jo-Jack and Burtrum. The airship stop was an open-air platform with a ramp leading up to it. They could see the red, cigar-shaped craft beginning its descent.

As it came down, the tactical OS dropped into Hanna's vision once again and zoomed in on something crawling over the top of the airship. It had four legs, each limb moving in isolation so that only one foot ever left the surface at a time. From the ground it looked small, but it must be the size of a large car. Earl squeezed her hand, and she looked over to see him staring urgently off into the crowd. Four large vehicles bearing the emblem of the Pacific States Autonomous Forces were making their way into the crowd. They were troop carriers that looked like buses with doors along the sides housing humanoid security drones. Out on the edge of the crowd Hanna could see mobile detainment cells being set up.

Crime in the Pacific States had become an anomaly—a statistical rounding error that didn't warrant local policing. Almost all emergency response was handled by paramedics, mental health professionals, social workers, or firefighting drones. However, there was still a considerable need for border security due to the socioeconomic situation of the Middle States and the Southwest. That security was handled by PSAF's fleet of armed robots. Most Seattleites would spend their whole lives never seeing them in person and only recognized them from reality VR shows. The loving mob of people had not registered the troop carriers yet, but their friends in the airship did and stopped its descent.

The drones jumped from the troop carriers and made their way into the crowd. They were grabbing people and pulling them towards he detainment cells. As this started, Hanna felt a tear in the mob's manufactured wellbeing. It rippled up from her stomach, ending with a catch in her throat. The whiplash of emotions sobered her in an instant and left tears in her eyes. The protective bubble of love and connection she'd been drunk on cracked open and the anxiety of her situation came flooding in. The stark contrast between the emotions was painful.

Then, like ice breaking on the surface of a lake she could feel fear radiating through the crowd. People were turning on each other and every person who had downloaded the OTAKU application was acting as a node in the network of growing terror.

"Uninstall the fucking application, Earl. It's amplifying the wrong feelings!"

Earl mumbled something to his OS and shook his head, trying to get his bearings. The closest troop carrier was between them and the way out. Earl began moving in that direction, but Hanna grabbed his arm.

"Hold on. Just give me a moment to look for another exit." He was confused but waited. Hanna took a breath and willed the tactical OS back into being. It hit her body first, a feeling of tweaked adrenaline and muscle support. Then, superimposed in her lenses was an overhead view of Seattle Center. The Space Needle at the center but also showing crowd movements and the PSAF carriers. A path was highlighted taking them away from the obvious exit. It led further into the mess before leading them out to a street on the far side of the grounds. Before going that way Hanna paused for another moment to look up at the airship.

The crab-walking robot still clung to it. Her OS zoomed in to reveal that it had punctured a hole in the airship. Yevgeny and Xin-Lao were already piloting the thing away from the scene, but it was clear they wouldn't make it far. It seemed like a perfect way for PSAF to capture the two of them away from the increasingly violent mob. She looked up at Earl's bewildered face.

"Okay, with me," she said and started in the direction of their escape route. Earl made a move to step in front of her, planning to plow a way through the crowd for them. It was turning ugly and just as they started moving a bottle flew toward his face. The familiar feeling of power that came with the jacket was back and before either of them could think Hanna, jumped up hitting the bottle out of the air with her forearm. "I'll lead," she said.

The jacket's enhancements were intoxicating. Her heightened senses, speed, and strength were all the more pronounced in the disoriented crowd. Hanna moved at a jog, knocking people out of their way, occasionally parrying a blow from some random asshole or deliberately kicking someone's legs out from under them as they attacked a fearful bystander. She found a rhythm and discovered an economy of movement as she forged through the mob. A step away from someone falling over became a step into another man as he swung a bike lock at her. She closed the space between them, tucking her shoulder under his armpit while grabbing his wrist to lift him off his feet and throw him to the ground. It was unbelievably satisfying, and she was a little bummed when they reached the edge of the plaza. Looking back to confirm that Earl was still with her, she found him speechless with his mouth open.

SEATTLE CENTER

The two of them stood at the edge of the crowd and before Earl could start to question her about her surprising abilities, they were distracted again by the scene unfolding in front of them.

People were freaking out as they were ripped from euphoria into panic. Groups were fighting one another, themselves, and the large humanoid PSAF drones. One of the drones must have been following them as Hanna had been kicking ass because it zeroed in on them, making its way through the crowd in their direction. Two incensed idiots climbed up on its back and it shook them off, like a dog trying to get dry.

Hanna had never seen a PSAF border control drone up close. They were big. The one converging on them didn't have a head and neck, just a few sturdy looking sensors in the front of its chest. Technology in the Pacific States had been developed to remain hidden. The inner workings of the world lived behind a thin veneer of faux surfaces and buried under the streets. So, it was jarring to see this robot with all its hydraulics, armor plating, and cameras exposed. Everything about it was intimidating. The mechanisms in its legs flexed as it neared, its movements clumsy but powerful. It raised an arm, pointing what they could only assume was some kind of weapon at them. Looking around, Earl found a mobility wheel laying on its side. Picking it like an empty cardboard box, he flung it at the PSAF drone and they both ran. Hanna heard the drone knock the wheel aside and start after them.

They ran for their lives, or at least from an undetermined period of incarceration. Then, over the pounding of blood in her ears, Hanna heard Jo-Jack's voice in her ear. "Keep moving. Go left around the next building. I've got a bike waiting for you there."

"Thank fucking God! I don't think we could have made it out with that thing after us." She pointed at her ear while looking at Earl, the universal sign for *I'm talking to someone else.*

"They're not designed for urban locomotion. Find things to jump over, or squeeze through," Jo-Jack said.

"Earl! We're going to split up and meet on the far side of that building. There will be a motorbike there. I need you to hop on it and it will take you to me. Okay?" Hanna yelled.

"Okay!" Earl veered left without looking back at her.

Hanna slowed her pace, making the PSAF drone focus on her as the two of them parted. She willed the tactical OS into full fight-or-flight, feeling adrenaline course through her body. The exhaustion left her legs and the jacket constricted around her torso protectively. She slowed to a stop and turned to face the drone.

It was running hard and stopped suddenly to keep itself from trampling her. It fell forward, landing on all fours and kept trotting along while its sensor group pivoted to keep looking at her. It came to a full stop and began the process of standing back up on two legs. Hanna started running again. The fraction of a second this gained her, along with the time it took for the drone to get up to running speed again, was enough for her to make it into an open green space with a children's playground. She hurdled a couple of benches, leaped through a jungle gym, and vaulted over a pirate ship before making it out the other side well ahead of the drone.

Without looking back, she could tell it was falling behind. Its heavy footsteps sounded farther and farther away. As she cleared the grass, Earl's massive frame rounded the corner of the old armory riding a vantablack motorcycle. She leaped on the seat behind him and held on to his torso as they escaped. The drone ran after them for a while but was no match for the bike once it found open road.

=

The bike brought them to one of the few remaining industrial pockets of South Lake Union. Jo-Jack was waiting with his convoy. The truck and its two trailers stood there featureless, reflecting none of the midday light. Hanna walked over to Jo-Jack and hugged him before introducing Earl. Then, to her surprise, Burtrum hopped out of the passenger seat.

"I wasn't sure you'd come," Hanna said.

"I gave you my contact key," he replied as though that answered everything.

"Still."

Jo-Jack cut back in. "We're briefed on the situation from your OS. There's not a lot of time."

"First things first. You'll need to go dark." Burtrum held out a silver bag a lot like the one Yevgeny had kept the phone in before unleashing the algo on the city that morning.

Hanna and Earl removed their lenses and tossed their storage bottles in the box.

"Now we didn't account for two of you, so I've only built one helmet," Burtrum said.

"I wasn't planning on an active role in whatever you all are about to do," Earl admitted.

"Probably for the best. I don't want you any deeper in this than you already are." Hanna squeezed his big bicep.

Burtrum pulled a motorcycle helmet out of the cab and handed it to Hanna. "I've designed it to scramble all visual identifiers. With this on, you will be anonymous."

"I really don't know how to thank you for coming all this way," Hanna said.

"In my experience, this is how friendship starts. Somebody does something kind for someone else." Burtrum gave her a hug. His rotund body felt nice against hers.

"When did you two have time to make this? Things only went sideways in the last twenty minutes." Then, before Jo-Jack could answer, she remembered. "Right, if everything has to go right for your plan to work, you have a shitty plan."

"I have something else for you." Jo-Jack gestured for Hanna to follow him to one of the trailers and they climbed inside.

"You sure you can do this?" he asked once they were alone

"No, but there's no one else. You two are already going above and beyond. It was a lot to ask you to smuggle them into Canada. Now that this is a rescue operation, it's up to me."

"I was actually asking whether you wanted to do it."

"I do."

"Okay, then you should take this." He handed her a small hoop reminding her of a gymnastics ring from her gym. On the side pointing away from her, a sharp spike protruded menacingly, under her fingers rested two triggers.

"This thing looks very illegal."

"Oh, yeah. You'll go away for a long time if you're caught with this. But that ship has already sailed, so just don't get caught. When you want to fire it, squeeze both triggers. Release the first trigger and the spike lets go of whatever you shot. Release the second trigger to retract the spike into the handle. It activates automatically when it penetrates electronics."

"And when you say, 'activates automatically'?"

"It's called a harpoon. It's an EMP device. It will brick a drone, car, or pretty much anything else in the modern world. Please, don't let it touch my bike." Jo-Jack strapped a holster for the harpoon to her right thigh, his hands touching her leg in a way she found distracting.

Hanna bent down and pulled his face into hers to kiss him.

"Thank you for coming."

WESTLAKE

The helmet, jacket, and bike worked together, creating a feeling that was greater than the sum of their parts. She was on the bike riding through traffic and from the moment she'd put the helmet on, she felt different. It was like the effect of the jacket times ten. There was no hesitation in her, only flawless reaction times and perfect situational awareness.

Hanna was in direct communication with the bike, driving it herself rather than relying on its autonomous controls. She threaded in and out of traffic, finding the tight gaps left between self-driving cars. Up ahead, some asshole was slowing everything down by insisting on manual control of his own vehicle. The ripples in traffic caused by his human reaction time were felt blocks away, jamming everything up at the intersection of Denny and Westlake.

"Probably best to give this thing a test," Hanna said to herself as she came up behind him pulling the harpoon from its holster on her thigh.

The ring's two triggers rested comfortably under her fingers. As she came within a couple of car lengths she raised it and pulled them. The spike on the harpoon shot out trailing a thin cord behind it and impaled the back of the idiot driver's car. The car went completely dead. She released the harpoon by letting go of one trigger and retracted the spike into the ring with the other. She flew past the dead vehicle leaving an even worse traffic jam in her wake.

Hanna could see the airship now. It had crashed by the water's edge on the west side of South Lake Union. Its nose was crumpled, semi-deflated, leaving the tail end floating up at an odd angle. PSAF crowd control drones were leaping from the side of a single troop carrier that was rolling to a stop. The crab walker that had punctured the blimp's hull was beside it holding the exit closed, preventing Xin-Lao and Yevgeny's escape. It was large up close, more like a walking tank than a car.

Hanna kept the bike at a decent speed and circled the scene taking stock of the situation. The drone carrier was accompanied by an aerial drone that hovered above the scene. As she came back for a second pass, the PSAF drones were forming a perimeter. She began to fire and retract the harpoon as she circled, taking one after another offline. Her movements were unnaturally fluid. It felt like watching someone else. She circled again and the aerial drone dove to intercept her. It began shooting, and everything slowed. Hard rubber bullets pounded the ground in front of the bike, forcing Hanna to make a sudden turn. The adrenaline cocktail being curated in her system by the jacket and helmet combo made it all happen in slow motion. She could see the projectiles hitting and bouncing off the ground. The bike's gyroscopes kept it from falling over, but they didn't keep Hanna in the seat during the turn. She tumbled off, landing hard on the ground, and the bike pulled away.

She landed on her side, managing to roll to her feet with the momentum. Looking down at her leg, Hanna saw blood but couldn't feel any pain. A group of PSAF drones were coming at her.

"Are you ready for extraction?" Jo-Jack said in her ear.

"Not yet. They're still trapped."

The closest drone pointed what looked like a club at her and a shot of compressed air knocked her to the ground. With a quick jump, it was on top of her, landing with its feet on either side of her chest. In its other hand it held a set of restraints.

Hanna stabbed the unextended spike of the harpoon right into what would have been its balls. The drone fell forward, powerless. Another one grabbed her by the arm, pulling her to her feet. She stabbed the spike into its chest and pulled it out, before turning to shoot it into another drone coming her way. She ran to avoid an air cannon blast from behind her and found her rhythm again, dropping drone after drone with the harpoon. Robot bodies were piling up around her. She turned to see the crab walker detach itself from the airship, letting the door swing open, and turn her way. She limped away from it. The thing must have been designed for crowd control, because it raised one of its legs, revealing a nozzle, and began to shoot orange foam at her. Some of it hit her boot and hardened, almost trapping her to the ground.

Without thinking Hanna looked up at the aerial drone, took aim, and shot the harpoon into it. She released the retraction trigger leaving the spike in and the harpoon's cable pulled her into the air. The aerial drone was hovering between her and the crab walker so the ascent flung her forward and up. Halfway, Hanna released the spike and flew through the air landing on top of the crab walker as the aerial drone fell lifeless to the pavement. Her body hit hard, and she almost rolled off, catching herself with a flailing hand. Hanging on for dear life as the big robot jerked this way and that, she stabbed frantically with the spike. It wouldn't pierce the armor.

As she climbed over its body looking for any exposed electronics, she saw Yevgeny peeking his head out of the airship door, holding the Faraday pouch. The crab walker saw him and started to lurch back in the direction of the airship. As it scuttled forward raising the foam-spraying leg, Hanna caught a glimpse of hydraulics where the leg connected to the shoulder and dove for them. The spike connected with the crab walker's insides, bringing it to a stop with one leg raised over Yevgeny's head.

"Now! Come get us now!" Hanna yelled.

Jo-Jack's convoy rolled in, scattering the remaining PSAF drones. Hanna ushered Yevgeny and Xin-Lao into the open back of a follow trailer and they all pulled away as more PSAF troop carriers arrived on scene. The convoy sped along Westlake Avenue towards I-5. Earl was in the trailer and the four of them looked out the back door in horror.

A single PSAF troop carrier was close behind and had drones crawling all over it. They were forming a chain from the front of the carrier to reach them. Hanna shot the spike over and over again, dropping one after the other to the road only to be replaced with the one behind it.

"Hang on!" she heard Jo-Jack say. "We can outrun them as soon as we hit the freeway!"

The growing robotic mass of limbs clambered over itself attempting to form a bridge between the carrier and the trailer. Hanna fended them off as best she could, but nothing worked. They began to grab hold of the trailer and one drone pulled itself inside. The four friends retreated, and Hanna shot the spike into the drone that made it into the trailer. As the spike hit its chest another drone behind the one she hit reached in and grabbed the harpoon cable, looping it around the arm of the dead one. As the dead drone fell off the trailer, it pulled the harpoon from Hanna's hand. Her weapon was gone.

Calmly, as though it had been their plan all along, Xin-Lao took the Faraday pouch from Yevgeny and walked to the rear of the trailer. Then they turned their back to the drones, holding the little pouch high for everyone to see and looked at Yevgeny, Earl, and Hanna.

"I love you."

Xin-Lao fell backwards into the arms of the PSAF drones. The teaming mass of robots collapsed in on itself enveloping them, pulling their body into the troop carrier with them. Moments later, Jo-Jack led the convoy onto the freeway finally pulling away from the pursuers.

Earl, Hanna, and Yevgeny looked at each other, speechless. As the convoy flew north toward the Canadian border, Yevgeny cried quietly in Earl's arms. Hanna followed his gaze down to his hands and saw that he was still holding the phone. He never put it back in the pouch.

EPILOGUE

"Xin-Lao's been totally erased. All their records, search history—everything is gone," Earl said.

It had been two weeks since they delivered Yevgeny to the Canadian border, essentially forcing him to follow through with his escape by insisting that it was what Xin-Lao sacrificed themself for. Hanna, Earl, Jo-Jack, and Burtrum had returned to Seattle with the convoy that same night. Hanna only kept it together long enough to get dropped off, insisting that Jo-Jack leave her alone and get out of the city. It was a demand she claimed she made for his safety but was actually motivated by her need to fall apart in private.

For the next couple of weeks, she barely slept and didn't eat enough. The hole Xin-Lao's disappearance left in her life was massively out of proportion to the length of time they had been close. Their relationship took place over the course of days, but Hanna felt like she had lost a dear friend and important lover. She ignored work while she grieved, telling her therapy cloud to keep her on mental health leave indefinitely. She was only shaken out of her dark place by a message asking if she was going to accept the promotion waiting for her when she returned to Moshi Moshi. At first, Hanna thought it was a mistake, but then remembered the joke she made to Tapeesa when she was negotiating the safe harbor for Yevgeny and Xin-Lao.

It dawned on her in that moment that Yevgeny must be safe since Big Water was paying out on their end of the deal. That realization was the crack in her depression that let some light in. Light that spread quickly and finally lifted her up out of bed and kicked her back into her regularly scheduled life.

Earl, it seemed, hadn't missed a beat in those two weeks she had been out of commission, telling Hanna all about the work he and Burtrum were doing to try and locate Xin-Lao. He just skipped over the part where he and Burtrum had somehow become close friends during that process but did find time to drop hints that he was thinking about moving off grid with Burtrum's tribe of hapticless friends.

Hanna and Earl sat eating the breakfast he made for them at the Sorcery Outlet before she was due back at work for the first time since hitting Mason.

"I feel terrible. I should have been looking for them with you two. I can't believe you've been out here doing shit while I was crying in my apartment," Hanna said.

"I think we have both been in shock and grieving in our own ways. Besides, we didn't find anything useful."

"Still..."

"Be gentle with yourself," he said, smiling at her. "Besides, I think it's best that you don't look into their disappearance if you'd like to continue on with the life you negotiated for yourself. Burtrum and I won't stop until we find them, but we have the luxury of being able to step outside of the system."

"So, you're leaving the city? And what? Going off the grid?" Hanna asked.

"Something like that. I'll keep this place for when I'm back in town. I own the building anyway, so I'll have to come around now and then."

"I'm sorry... Earl, are you rich?"

"You and I never really got know each other, huh?" he said. "Let's make time for that soon. But for now, you should probably get a look at what's been going on across the city while you've been cocooned in your home."

Hanna held his giant frame tightly as she stood in the door on the way out.

"Take care of yourself," he whispered in her ear and followed it with a peck on the cheek.

=

Hanna walked through First Hill into downtown on her way to work. She'd kept her lenses out and her haptics off for the weeks she'd been at home. She didn't want to be tempted to turn the feelings down. She didn't want to forget what it felt like to miss Xin-Lao. Hanna had given the jacket back to Jo-Jack when he left and being without it left her even more raw and exposed. She was beginning to suspect that the feeling of losing it was also contributing to her reluctance to face the world.

Now knowing that she'd need lenses for work, she pulled the bottle from her bag and squirted one into each eye. Her OS eased her back into mixed reality, slowly dialing up the haptics in her clothes as she was assaulted by mixed reality ads again for the first time in weeks. The usual perfectly curated signage came along, showing her things she didn't realize she was thinking about buying until she saw them. But something felt different. There was a subtle compulsion missing. The change was so slight that she wouldn't have been able to tell if she hadn't been looking for it. Each ad lacked an emotional appeal. They fell flat in some way that made them easier to ignore. The algo wasn't pushing emotional experiences at her anymore. It would never be admitted to, but Xin-Lao and Yevgeny's exhibit had done it. The removal of the emotional influence in ads was proof of their theory. Hanna felt like she was breaking the surface of the water she had been submerged in her whole life. She felt excited for life, free to seek out whatever unfettered obsessions came next. Was it possible that Alphabet's soft molding of the world's emotional state was responsible for the loss of otaku over the generations?

Hanna walked by two people as they greeted each other, clearly on a first date in a cafe. As they sat down, they both paused to remove their lenses, smiling at each other as they put the lens bottles away. Hanna heard one of them speak.

"So, tell me about yourself."

ABOUT THE AUTHOR

Casey Milone (he/they) is a career-long copywriter and creative director whose past work includes rebranding an airline, launching consumer electronics, and messaging strategy to sell AI. He now runs a marketing agency and lives with his wife and schnauzer in Victoria, British Columbia.

To check out the generative artwork that has been created alongside this book and learn about upcoming projects go to: www.caseymilone.com

ACKNOWLEDGEMENTS

I would first like to acknowledge the many, many people who have put up with my writing over the years during which it still sucked. This includes but is not limited to past employers, friends, and family. Each of you took the time to read things I wrote that I would be embarrassed to share now.

This work would not have been possible without the ongoing collaboration of my dear friend and vocational spirit animal Samuel Stubblefield. Without the invaluable editing of Ian Cockfield and Hannah VanVels it would not have seen the light of day. And in the absence of the unwavering support of my wife I would not have found the courage to publish.